Yuri Trifonov was born in 1925 into the privileged world of high-ranking Soviet society. His father, however, one of the Old Bolsheviks who had joined the Party before the Revolution, disappeared in the Stalinist purges, and his name was expunged from Party history. Trifonov, after having won a Stalin prize for an early novel, devoted ten years of his life to rehabilitating his father's name. It was not until he was forty-four that he found his true voice as a writer. There followed throughout the 1970s his series of short novels, culminating with *Another Life* and *The House on the Embankment*, that established him as one of the foremost novelists of his generation. He died suddenly on March 28, 1981.

Yuri Trifonov

THE HOUSE ON THE EMBANKMENT

Translated from the Russian by Michael Glenny

First published in Great Britain in Abacus by
Sphere Books Ltd 1985
30–32 Gray's Inn Road, London WC1X 8JL
Copyright © Druzhba Narodov Magazine 1976
English language translation Copyright © 1983 by Michael Glenny
First published in the United States of America 1983 by Simon and
Schuster, Inc. in one volume with *Another Life*.

Set in Times

Printed and bound in Great Britain by
Cox & Wyman Ltd, Reading

Not one of those boys is alive today. Some were killed in the war, some died from sickness, some disappeared without a trace, while others, though still alive, have turned into different people; and if by some magic means those different people were to meet their past selves – in their cotton twill shirts and canvas shoes – they would no longer know what to say to them. I fear, in fact, that they would not even guess they were meeting themselves. Well, to hell with them, if they're so imperceptive. They have no time to spare, anyway; they have to hurry on, to swim with the current, paddling with their hands, farther and farther, faster and faster, day after day, year after year: the shores change, the hills recede, the forests thin out and vanish, the sky darkens, the cold sets in, they have to hurry, hurry – and they no longer have the strength to look back at what is behind them and fading away like a cloud on the edge of the horizon.

On one of the intolerably hot August days of 1972 – Moscow that summer was suffocating in the sultry heat and smoky haze, and it was Glebov's bad luck to have to spend time in town because they were expecting to move into a new apartment – Glebov drove out to a furniture store in a new district, somewhere near the Koptevsky market, and there a funny thing happened. He met an old friend from way back – and he forgot the man's name. Glebov had come here to get a table. He had been given a tip-off about the table: the people who tipped him off didn't know exactly where it was at the moment – that was a secret, but they described it – antique, with inlaid medallions, a perfect match for the mahogany chairs that Marina had bought a year ago for the new flat. They said there was someone called Yefim who worked in the furniture shop near the Koptevsky market and who knew where the table was. Glebov drove there after lunch in the grilling heat, parked his car in the shade and walked over to the shop. On the pavement in front of the entrance, among heaps of rubbish and torn wrapping paper, were stacks of furniture that had just been delivered or were waiting to be picked up – wardrobes, sofas, all kinds of shiny plastic-finished junk – surrounded by a milling crowd of customers, taxi drivers and scruffy-looking loafers who would do anything for a three-rouble tip. Glebov asked where Yefim

1

was to be found. The answer was: at the back, in the yard. Glebov walked through the shop, where the stuffiness and the reek of spirit-based varnish made it almost impossible to breathe, and went out through a narrow door into the backyard. A workman was dozing in a spot of shade by the wall, squatting on his haunches. Glebov said to him, "You're not Yefim, are you?"

The workman raised a bleary eye, frowned and just managed to purse his lips until a contemptuous dimple formed on his chin, which was supposed to mean 'No'. From that dimple and from something else indefinable Glebov suddenly realised that this wretched, heat-dazed and drink-sodden furniture porter had once been a friend of his. It was not his eyes that told him this, but an inner sensation that felt like a slight thump. But the terrible thing was that although he knew this man perfectly well, he had completely forgotten his name. As he stood there in silence, swaying slightly back and forth in his squeaky sandals, he stared at the workman and racked his brains to remember, bringing a whole era of his life suddenly flooding back. But what *was* his name? It was something unusual and funny, and at the same time childish, a unique name. His nameless friend was settling down to doze again; he pulled his cap down over his nose, and his mouth fell open as he tipped his head back.

Disturbed, Glebov walked away and peered around here and there looking for Yefim, then went back into the shop, where he asked several people if they knew where he might be. No one did and Glebov was advised to wait, but he could not. Mentally cursing these unhelpful people, he went out again into the burning heat of the yard, where he had been so amazed and perplexed by Shulepa. But of course, that was it – Shulepa! It had been their nickname for Lev Shulepnikov. He remembered hearing some time ago that Shulepa had dropped out of sight and had probably ended up somewhere on the rubbish heap. But had he really ended up *here*? In a furniture shop? He wanted to say a friendly word to him, to inquire as an old pal what had happened to him, and at the same time ask him about Yefim.

'Lev . . .' said Glebov rather uncertainly as he approached the man, who was still squatting on his haunches in the same patch of shade but no longer dozing. He was watching some activity at the far end of the yard, a cigarette between his lips.

Then Glebov said, louder and more boldly: 'Shulepa!'

The man gave Glebov another bleary-eyed stare and turned away. Of course it was Lev Shulepnikov – only very old-looking, haggard and battered by life, with a greying moustache, greatly changed in appearance yet having somehow kept a trace of his old obstinate, cheeky and absurdly arrogant self. Should he give him some money to get himself a hair of the dog? Glebov fumbled in his trousers' pocket, feeling the coins there. He could easily give him, say, four roubles, if he asked for it; but the man paid him no attention and Glebov felt embarrassed, thinking he had been mistaken and this creature wasn't Shulepnikov at all. But at the same instant, in a burst of irritation, he blurted out, rudely and in the patronising tone he used when talking to shop girls and waiters: 'Hey, don't you recognise me? Lev!'

Shulepnikov spat out his cigarette end, and without a glance at Glebov stood up and lurched towards the far end of the yard, where some men were starting to unload a container. Feeling an unpleasant sense of shock, Glebov wandered out to the street. He was amazed not only by Lev Shulepa's appearance and his present wretched condition, but also by the fact that Lev *had not wanted* to recognise him. Some people might have reason to resent Glebov, but Lev was not one of them. Anyway, it hadn't been the fault of Glebov or of anyone else; the times had been to blame, and you couldn't exactly take it out on the times. Again he had a sudden memory of the distant past, of mean and stupid things; the house on the embankment, snow-covered backyards, electric lights strung on bare wires, fights in the snowdrifts by a brick wall. His recollection of Shulepa was made up of flaky, disparate layers that refused to merge into a coherent image, but that particular memory – in the snowdrifts beside a brick wall, when they had fought until they drew blood, until one of them gasped, 'I give up,' when afterwards in the huge warm house they had blissfully sipped hot tea from fragile china cups – that, no doubt, had been real. Still, one could never be sure: reality looks different at different times.

If he were to be honest with himself, Glebov hated *that* time, because it had been the time of his childhood.

As he told the story to Marina that evening, he found himself getting indignant and irritable, not because he had

3

met an old friend who refused to recognise him, but because he had to deal with such irresponsible people as Yefim, who promise something and then either forget or knowingly let you down, so that an antique marquetry table gets snapped up by someone else. They drove out to spend the night at their *dacha*, which they found in a state of alarm. Despite the late hour, Glebov's in-laws had not yet gone to bed: his daughter Margot, it appeared, had ridden off that morning on the back of Tolmachev's motorbike, had not phoned home all day and it was nine o'clock before she had called up to say she was in some artist's studio on Vernadsky Prospect. She had begged them not to worry, and Tolmachev would be bringing her back by midnight. Glebov burst out in fury: 'On a motorbike? At night? Why didn't you tell the little fool not to be crazy, to come back at once, this minute . . .?' The in-laws, like a comic old couple in a play, mumbled something stupid and irrelevant:

'I was watering the flowers like you said to, Vadim, when the water supply was cut off. So maybe you should ask the management . . .'

Glebov waved his hand in irritation and went upstairs to his study. Even now, in the late evening, it was as hot and stuffy as ever. Dry, dead leaves were drifting in from the garden. Glebov took his medicine and lay down fully dressed on the couch, thinking how today – provided all was well and she actually returned alive – he must talk to his daughter about Tolmachev and make her see what a nonentity this young man was. At twelve-thirty came the pop-popping of a motorbike, followed by the sound of voices downstairs; Glebov was relieved to recognise his daughter's high-pitched, twittering voice. At once all his anxiety evaporated, the desire to give his daughter a talking-to disappeared and he began to make up a bed for himself on the couch, knowing that his wife would now stay up into the small hours chattering with Margot.

The two women, however, burst noisily and unceremoniously into his study. The light was still on and Glebov was wearing only his white underpants, with one foot on the carpet and the other on the couch as he snipped at his toenails with a little pair of scissors.

All the blood seemed to have gone from his wife's face and

4

she said plaintively: 'Do you realise she's going to marry Tolmachev?'

'What?' Glebov looked shocked, but he was not really shocked; it was just that Marina looked so extremely unhappy. 'When?'

'In twelve days' time, when he comes back from a business trip,' Margot gabbled breathlessly, the speed of her diction stressing the categorical and irrevocable nature of the impending event. She smiled as she spoke, while the slightly puffy cheeks, the little nose, the spectacles and her mother's black boot-button eyes that made up her immature face shone and glistened, blind with happiness. Margot flung herself at her father and kissed him. Glebov caught the smell of liquor. He hastily slid under the sheet. He didn't like his grown-up daughter seeing him in his underpants; what was worse, she was not in the least embarrassed by it and even seemed not to notice her father's appearance. In fact, at this particular moment she was not seeing anything at all; her whole behaviour was completely infantile. And this little fool was intending to launch out into an independent life with some man. Or rather, with some no-good layabout. Glebov asked her:

'What business trip? You don't mean to tell me Tolmachev has a job?'

'Of course he has. He's a salesman in a bookshop.'

'In a bookshop? A salesman?' Glebov was so astonished that he flung his arms out from under the sheet. This was news to him, no doubt some underhand trick. 'Why haven't I heard about this before? You told me he was an artist. You even showed me some of his pictures . . . still lifes, candlesticks and an iron . . .'

'No, she did tell you where he works. Yes, she did,' Marina said, anxious to be fair. 'But that's not the point . . .'

'Oh, Mother, how I love you both!' Margot burst out, kissing her mother and laughing. 'Daddy, you look so pale. How are you feeling?'

'And where is your fiancé at this moment?'

'Dad – please – you're not to worry about *anything*.'

'Margot answer me. Where are you proposing to live?'

Salesman in a bookshop. It could hardly be worse. It was a long time since he had seen a look of such sublime happiness, heard such inane laughter. Giggling, Margot said, 'Is that really so important?'

'But your father and I want to know.'

'Oh, you want to know, do you? Are you devoured by curiosity?' More laughter. 'Well, suppose we say . . . here. Is that bad? Will you let us?'

'You mean you'll get the bus into Moscow? Get up at five o'clock every morning?'

'Mama, none of that matters.'

Suddenly, both women were gone. Minutes later, Glebov listened as the female voices came floating up from below, joined by the muted burbling of his father-in-law and mother-in-law. Glebov's heart ached with premonitions of change, and he decided to take a sleeping tablet. Suddenly he had a happy thought: 'Maybe it won't be so bad after all. Let things take their course. As they always do. Those two will probably separate after a year anyway, and that'll be that.' And he started to think about something else.

At about one o'clock in the morning the telephone rang. Half asleep, Glebov could feel his anger rising, his heartbeat getting faster, and then, nimble as a young man, he jumped up from the couch and almost flung himself at the telephone on his desk: he must reach it before Margot picked up the downstairs receiver. He'd give that cheeky young slob an earful. He was sure it was Tolmachev calling.

The voice, however, was unknown. It sounded slurred, coarse and insolent: 'Hullo, Dunya, happy New Year . . . Don't recognise me, eh?' croaked the offensive voice. 'One moment you recognise me, next you don't. What an arsehole . . . What's the time? Just after one . . . hell, that's nothing. We intellectuals aren't in bed yet, are we? We're still up, solving problems. I'm sitting here with some fellow . . . Hey, d'you remember the sheath knives I used to have?'

'Yes, I do,' said Glebov. And he did remember: there were five of them, all of different sizes. The smallest was no bigger than a cigarette. Lev used to bring them to school and show off with them; he also had had a gleaming nickel-plated revolver with a bone handle, just like a real one.

Marina came into the study and flashed him a frightened, inquiring look: 'Who is it?' Glebov winked at her and signalled that it was nothing important. But for some odd reason he was glad Shulepnikov had rung up.

'All right, that's it then. Sleep well, comrade. Sorry I disturbed you. It took me three hours to find your phone number through Enquiries . . . Are you listening? When you saw me today I didn't want you to know I recognised you. "What the fuck use are you to me," I thought. I really used to dislike you . . . Hey, did you hear that, Vadim, for Christ's sake? I mean what I say: I really disliked you.'

'But why?' asked Glebov, yawning.

'God knows. You never did me any harm, really. I suppose you must be a doctor or a professor or some kind of big wheel now, the cherry on top of a cake of shit. I couldn't care less, though. Doesn't bother me. I'm out of the rat race now . . . But when I got home I started thinking: "Why did I give old Vadim Glebov the cold shoulder, huh? Maybe he wanted some piece of junk, and I could've helped him. Then when he comes next time I may not be there." They're sending me you-know-where for three years . . .'

'Oh God,' thought Glebov. 'In his condition, he'll be dead by then . . .'

'Lev, please, call me tomorrow.'

'No, I won't call you tomorrow. Only today. What are you, a minister? Call me tomorrow, indeed! Who the hell d'you think you are? You must be out of your mind to talk to me like that. I've just spent three hours tracking down your phone number, him and me . . . He's a foreign diplomat, great chap . . . He got your number through Enquiries at the Ministry of Foreign Affairs. Say, Vadim, d'you remember my mother?'

Glebov said he did remember her and was about to add that he also remembered Lev's father – no, his stepfather – or rather, his two stepfathers. But there was a click in the earpiece, followed by the buzz of the dialling tone.

Marina was still looking frightened.

'Just some idiot . . . Actually it was the chap I saw at the furniture shop this afternoon.' Glebov was standing barefoot beside his desk and staring thoughtfully at the telephone. 'What a berk, though . . . What the hell did he want to ring me up for?'

Almost a quarter of a century ago, when Vadim Alexandrovich Glebov was not yet balding and fat, with breasts like a woman's, flabby thighs, a big paunch and sloping shoulders, which obliged him to have his suits tailor-made instead of buying them off the rack (while his jacket size was fifty-two he could barely squeeze into trousers of size fifty-six, and sometimes had to get a pair of fifty-eights); when he did not yet have bridgework in both his upper and lower jaws; when the doctors had not yet noted the irregularities in his ECG that indicated cardiac insufficiency and stenosis of the coronary arteries; when he was not yet a martyr to morning heartburn, dizzy spells and general listlessness; when his liver was still working normally and he could eat fatty foods and greasy meat, drink as much wine and vodka as he liked without fear of the consequences; when he did not yet know that pain in the small of his back which was caused by stress, extreme cold or God knows what else; when he was not afraid to swim across the Moscow River at its widest point; when he could play volleyball for four hours without a rest; when he was thin and bony and fast on his feet, with long hair and round spectacles that made him look like a young nineteenth-century revolutionary; when he was often broke and worked as a loader at the goods station or chopped firewood in suburban backyards; when near-starvation had brought with it the possible onset of tuberculosis, luckily averted by being sent to the Crimea; when his father, his Aunt Paula and his grandmother were still alive and they all lived together in one room on the second floor of that little house on the embankment, in which six other families also lived and shared eight tables in the kitchen; when he loved singing songs with girls; when he wasn't called Vadim Alexandrovich but Glebych or Daddy-Long-Legs; when tortured by insomnia and the wretched inadequacy of youth, he dreamed of all the things that later came to him – but which brought him no joy because achieving them used up so much of his strength and so much of that irreplaceable something that is called life: in those days, almost a quarter of a century ago, there had been Professor Ganchuk, there had been Sonya, Anton, and Lev Shulepnikov, all of them Vadim's neighbours. There had also been other people who gradually disappeared; and there had been himself, totally unlike his present self, which was large but as unprepossessing as a slug. And Marina was as yet nowhere in sight.

Now Marina was sitting on the verandah in the shade of the

birch trees, carefully writing in her childish hand on the little white paper drumheads stretched tight over the tops of glass jars and fastened by thread around the necks of the jars: 'Gooseberry 72', 'Strawberry 72'. Anton had died long ago and Sonya, too, was gone. No one knew what had become of Professor Ganchuk; most likely he was dead too, and even if he were alive, he might as well be dead. Lev Shulepnikov was squatting in a patch of shade in the backyard of a furniture shop, propping up the wall, with a cigarette between his teeth, dozing and dreaming: always the same dreams – dreams of spacious rooms with high ceilings and the huge orange-coloured lampshades of the thirties . . .

It was like a play: first act, second act, third act, eighteenth act. In each act the characters are slightly changed. But years, decades pass between the acts. Act Two began when Shulepnikov turned up at their post-graduate institute (emerging out of nowhere in that natural way that is possible only in the first half of one's life, when everything seems to happen with ease and by design) in Glebov's third year. The business with Ganchuk and all the rest took up the fourth year and part of the fifth. From the very first Shulepnikov stood out among the other students – explicable, no doubt, by the offstage presence of his stepfather, who wielded enormous influence. Few of the students knew this, though of course it was well known to Glebov and Sonya to whom Lev Shulepnikov was simply good old Shulepa. The others saw him as a clever dick, very knowing and hell-bent on making a rapid and successful career: he was on this committee and that committee, had a finger in every pie and took his pick of all the best-looking girls. In reality he was nothing but a bullshit artist pure and simple, but it took them some time to find this out, and at first he annoyed a lot of people. Once, a big hefty Ukrainian from Kharkov called Smyga came up to Vadim in the corridor and said:

'Look here, Glebov, weren't you in school with this Shitupnikov character?'

Glebov said, 'Yes, I was, but there's no need to make tasteless jokes by mangling people's names.'

'All right, we'll leave his name alone, and we'll mangle his face instead,' promised Smyga. 'Tell Mr Shitface to keep his sweaty hands off the girls in our year. Or else we'll give him the treatment.'

9

A few days later Smyga appeared in the lecture hall with a swollen face, as though he had a dental abscess. With genuine astonishment Lev explained what had happened: 'This elephant attacked me in the gents and started shouting that he'd warned me but I hadn't paid any attention. He went on yelling at me, so I used some unarmed combat techniques and knocked him down. He smashed one of the toilets with his thick head.'

At first Glebov did not believe him, knowing that Lev was a confirmed liar, but he later discovered that the toilet really had been broken, after which he not only believed that Smyga had indeed been cruelly humiliated but he also believed all the other fantastic tales that Shulepnikov told about his life. There was, for instance, the story of how during the war he had been through some special, top-secret training school where they were taught to shoot, to throw knives, to kill with their bare hands and to speak foreign languages; they were then sent on mysterious missions far behind the German lines, but Lev had been demobilised early when he developed a stomach ulcer. There were reasons to doubt the truth of this story, because Shulepnikov spoke very bad German, was not much good at knife throwing, was generally loud-mouthed and indiscreet and lied about trivial things – none of which fitted in with the image he tried to create. Glebov finally decided that Lev probably had, in fact, been sent to this top-secret school (his stepfather had no doubt fixed it) and had aimed to become a sort of Lawrence of Arabia, but for some reason he had not made the grade. Smyga, who had so hated Lev, became his most devoted henchman and sycophant; this took place a year later, when his stepfather gave Lev a captured German Volkswagen as a present, and Lev would roll up to classes in this cherry-red Beetle, which made all the poor students so envious that it deprived them of the power of speech. Smyga followed Lev wherever he went, ran errands for him and introduced him to all the girls that had once belonged in his preserve.

In those days – the zenith of Lev's chequered and devious career – one's attitude to Lev Shulepnikov could only be expressed in two ways: servile devotion or spiteful envy. Glebov, Lev's oldest friend, was never his slave, even in junior school, where some boys are so apt to toady and fawn on others who are strong and rich; in the institute, too, he had preferred not to be one of Lev's clique of flatterers, although the temptation to do so had been there. A cloud of hangers-on had revolved around Shulepnikov, who had led a special sort of life – houses in the country, cars, theatre people, sports. It was the time when ice hockey (then known as 'Canadian hockey', or simply 'Canada') was just being popularised in the Soviet Union. It was fashionable – and still fairly exclusive – to be an ice-hockey fan; the stadium seats always contained a liberal sprinkling of women in Persian lamb coats and men in overcoats with beaver collars. Shulepnikov used to be seen around with some of the star players in the Air Force team. Although Glebov was intermittently attracted to this sophisticated lifestyle, he also saw it as phony and ultimately boring, and while Lev always remained generously well disposed towards him for old times' sake, Glebov kept his distance. This came not only from a slightly touchy unwillingness to be the tenth spoke in someone else's wheel, but also from his innate caution, which he sometimes utilised without the slightest apparent reason, by pure instinct. In an expansive moment Lev would say, 'Glebych, you're in demand!' This meant that one of Lev's girls had noticed Glebov, and had heard something about him or wanted to meet him (there was nothing odd in this; in those days quite a few girls were attracted to Glebov). Lev, of course, might have been exaggerating and the girl might not have asked to meet Glebov at all; it was just Lev offering him a taste of the joys of life. Lev was by nature a sociable creature. Glebov, however, always invented reasons to decline the offer; he was expecting Sonya, he had a date with Sonya, Sonya was ill. In reality this was his secret mechanism of self-preservation at work, which was amazing, because no one in those days could have guessed at the disasters that lay ahead.

But there was also something else, a feeling that Glebov could never quite throw off, that tortured him throughout those years, starting from a very early age – an aching, deeply rooted sense of resentment. His efforts to combat it or to rise above it always failed. It was like a chronic disease: at times severe, at times imperceptible, at other times so intense as to be unbearable. Why was it, for instance, that the good things in life simply fell into some people's laps, as though ordained by some higher being, whereas he, Glebov, always had to

11

struggle for everything, could attain his desires only by the sweat of his brow, by straining every muscle and sinew, only to find that, having gained whatever it was, his nerves were in shreds and his muscles stiff as dried leather? This pain – perhaps the best name for it was 'agony from the unfairness of things' – had begun long ago, probably in the third or fourth form, when Shulepa moved into the big block of flats – the house on the embankment. Glebov, by contrast, lived in the same two-storey house in which he had been born.

Alongside the huge grey block with its thousand windows giving it the look of a whole town, among the backyards, behind a church surrounded by stone ruins sticking to it like fungus to a tree stump, there nestled a slightly lopsided house with a roof that sagged in places, with four pilasters along its façade, known to the inhabitants of the surrounding streets as the 'Deryugin house'; Deryugin Street was also the name of the alley in which stood this beautiful house that was slightly askew. The vast grey pile next door towered over the street and kept the sun off it in the morning, while in the evening radio voices and gramophone music floated down from above. Up there in those lofty storeys, it seemed, a life went on that was utterly different from life in the small house below, painted yellow in keeping with centuries-old tradition. There was *unfairness* for you! Some people were never aware of it, some were indifferent to it, while others regarded it as right and proper, but for Glebov it was a source of burning resentment from his childhood onwards – perhaps a kind of envy, perhaps something else. His father had worked as a foreman-chemist in an old sweet factory, while his mother had done countless jobs without ever having a real occupation: she had been a seamstress, had worked in various offices, and had sold tickets in a cinema. Her job in that cinema, a shabby little place in a back street across the Moscow River, was the source of no little pride to Glebov, because it endowed him with one enormous advantage: he could see any film without having to pay, and occasionally, during the daytime when the auditorium was almost empty, he was even allowed to bring a friend or two with him – always provided, of course, that his mother was in a good mood.

This privilege was the foundation of Glebov's influence in his school class, and he used it sparingly and cleverly: he would invite boys whose friendship he wanted to cultivate or from whom he expected something in return; some he would tantalise with promises for a long time before inviting them, while there were some villains whom he would deprive of his bounty altogether. On this basis Glebov's power – well, if not power, then authority – lasted unchallenged until Lev Shulepa appeared on the scene. Lev moved into the big block of flats from somewhere in the suburbs, or maybe even from another city. He made an instant impression because he wore leather shorts. From the first he had an arrogant air; he would gaze at everyone with a lazy, contemptuous look in his blue eyes, he never started a conversation and he shared a bench with a girl. His leather shorts squeaked unbearably during school. Some of the other boys decided to teach him a lesson, or rather to take him down a peg. Or more precisely still – to humiliate him. There was a form of initiation known as 'ohoho': the victim would be lured to the backyard, where a gang of boys would fling themselves on him with cries of 'Ohoho!' and pull off his trousers. It promised to be great fun: they would yank off his amazingly squeaky leather shorts, and while he struggled and shouted the girls, who had been told in advance, would be watching it all from a window. Glebov egged the others on to deal with Shulepa, whom he did not like – in general he disliked anyone who lived in the big house – but at the last moment he decided not to take part. Perhaps he felt slightly ashamed. He looked on from a doorway that opened on to the back staircase.

After school, Lev was enticed into the backyard. There were five of them – a boy whose nickname was 'The Bear', Syava, Manyunya and two others – who surrounded Lev and started an argument; suddenly The Bear, the strongest boy in the form, grabbed Lev around the neck and flung him prone in a single jerk, while the rest threw themselves on him with cries of 'Ohoho!' Lev fought back, lashing out with his feet, but they inevitably overcame him, rolled him over onto his back, and someone sat on his chest. Suddenly there was a loud bang, as though a car tyre had burst. At once all five leapt aside, and Lev got to his feet. Still wearing his leather shorts, he was holding a pistol. He fired another shot into the air. There was a smell of powder smoke. It was a moment of horror. Glebov felt his legs sagging underneath him. The Bear raced towards him with eyes staring, pushed him aside and ran upstairs, leaping several steps at a time.

13

It later turned out that Shulepnikov had a toy pistol, a beautiful foreign model that fired special caps and made a noise like the shot from a real pistol. Shulepnikov emerged from the incident with great prestige, while his attackers were disgraced and subsequently made every possible effort to make peace and become friends with the owner of the remarkable cap pistol. Anyone possessing such a weapon could rule the roost in the backyards along the embankment. It was easier for Glebov to make up to Shulepa than for the others; he had not, after all, taken part in the attack. Shulepnikov showed no vindictiveness and seemed satisfied that the boys now tried to ingratiate themselves with him and were prepared to pay dearly for the chance to fire a shot from his pistol. But the matter didn't end as simply as that. Suddenly the headmaster appeared together with the director of studies and a policeman, and he shouted that these young 'gangsters' must be punished. The head was unrecognisable: he was shouting – that had never happened before – he was pale, his cheeks shook and he was in a vengeful mood. The director of studies said that what had happened was obviously an act of premeditated terror. The policeman stood there in silence, but his mere presence made everyone feel uncomfortable.

The head demanded to know the names of the attackers. Shulepnikov refused to name them; he said he had not been able to see who they were: they had pounced suddenly and then run away with equal speed. The head called two more such meetings but without the policeman. The headmaster's name was Bagsunder, and people thought that this strange name derived from the fact that he had bags under his eyes. He had a long white face and puffy, white half-moons under his lower eyelids. He fidgeted nervously and never sat quietly on his chair like the other teachers but paced back and forth in front of the blackboard like a clockwork toy. No one liked the form mistress, a thin woman nicknamed 'The Tube', but they all felt sorry for the head because he looked so harried.

'My friends, I beg you to show courage. Courage lies not in keeping silent but in speaking out.' His white face and stammering voice spoke of anything but courage. For all their sympathy for this worried old man, however, the class kept silent, as did Shulepa. He later told the others that his father had punished him by locking him for a whole evening in the

14

bathroom, which was dark and alive with cockroaches. And he had demanded names. But Lev refused to divulge a single name.

Thus from having been marked down for public humiliation, Shulepa was transformed into a hero. It was probably after this episode – the leather shorts, the cap pistol and Lev's heroic behaviour (one girl even wrote a poem in his honour) – that Glebov first began to feel that leaden, sickening resentment in his innermost soul. Because, he dimly felt, one person shouldn't have *everything* handed to him on a platter. This feeling was, if you like, a protest by nature herself – or nemesis. Later, Lev Shulepnikov was to feel that same nemesis, to feel the teeth of the dragon on his own wretched skin; but in those days, in the half-dream of childhood, no one could have imagined that one day everything would be turned upside down. Only Glebov sensed something – impossible now to say exactly what it was – something disturbing, like the muffled voices of the waking world heard in sleep. No, envy is far from being the petty, squalid emotion that it is made out to be: envy is a part of nature's protest, a signal that perceptive souls should be able to pick up. But none are so unfortunate as those stricken with envy; and there was no more crushing misfortune than that which overcame Glebov at the moment that should have been his triumph.

In the little cinema where his mother worked they were showing an old picture called *The Blue Express*, full of bloody adventures, shooting and murder. All the kids were longing to see it, but for some reason children were not allowed in. Glebov of course was admitted by his mother. The picture was incredibly exciting: for an hour and a half Glebov sat on his tip-up seat shivering as though from a chill. He naturally had to see the film several more times, and so began the period of his ascendancy and undisputed dominion, because except through him there was no way his school mates could hope to see this marvellous film. The plot centred around an attack on a Red train by the Whites, who massacred the women, old men and children but were in the end beaten by the Reds. The shooting and hand-to-hand fighting took place on the open platforms at each end of the passenger coaches, on the roofs and underneath the coaches as the train raced along at full speed. Few grown-ups seemed to want to see this film, so the little auditorium was practically empty during the daytime.

Glebov would choose one or two of the more worthy applicants, making his selection with great care; he would announce his decision after school, and then they would race headlong over the bridge in order to get to the cinema in time for the start of the afternoon showing. His mother could let in four or five at a time, but Glebov did not throw his favours around too generously; there was no hurry. He hoped that Shulepa, too, would ask him, would beg like the others, but Lev showed no interest in the film. One day he said off-handedly: 'I've seen it a hundred times already!'

This was, of course, a lie. During school Glebov would enjoy himself considering the various petitioners: one had offered him a whole set of French colonials with a stamp album thrown in for good measure; Manyunya had promised that his father would take them both to the races. There were other offers – and there were even threats. One girl had written him a note promising to kiss him if he took her to the film. This note greatly excited Glebov. He had never received notes from girls before and he had never been kissed. The girl's name was Dina Kalmykova, nicknamed 'Lampshade'. She was rather fat, with very red cheeks, dark brown eyes and black eyebrows; as she was not particularly pretty, Glebov had never paid her any attention before, but from then on he was to remember her all his life.

When he received her note, Glebov felt a momentary stab of hot fear. He was afraid to move, and even more afraid to turn around and look – Dina sat two rows behind him. His first action was to tear the note into tiny pieces. Then he began feverishly to consider what to do. He could, of course, have said to her: 'I'll take you to the film, but you don't have to kiss me.' But that would perhaps have sounded rude. She was really very plump, a regular fatty in fact, although she was very light on her feet. In PT classes she ran faster than any of the other girls, and she was good at walking along the beam and at rope climbing. She wore a pair of voluminous raspberry-coloured shorts with frills around the bottom of the legs; someone said they looked like a couple of lampshades, and that was how she got her nickname.

If the note had been sent by Svetlana Kirillova or Sonya Ganchuk, Glebov would have been much more excited. Glebov thought Svetlana was beautiful; she held herself proudly, she was slim and lithe, with dark-red plaits, and she always looked as if she was keeping an important secret that no one else knew. Sonya Ganchuk, on the other hand, did not attract him with beauty but with something else. Perhaps it was the fact that her father, Professor Ganchuk, was a hero of the Civil War, and on the walls of his study, where Sonya had once secretly taken Glebov, hung daggers, guns and a Turkish scimitar. If only Svetlana or Sonya had promised to kiss him. But Dina Lampshade put him in a dilemma.

Even so, choosing a minute during break when Dina was alone – she was standing with her back to the window, smiling and gazing up at the ceiling – he went up to her and muttered, 'We can go today if you like. Walrus and Chemist are coming too . . .' He paused, then added: 'That is, of course, if you want to.'

'Yes, I want to,' said Dina, continuing to smile and stare at the ceiling.

'Only don't delay, or we'll be late. It's at two-thirty. Put your things on right away after school and we'll run. All right?' He spoke briskly, with no hint of sentiment.

The best part of *The Blue Express*, with all the shooting, was still to come, when Dina whispered in Glebov's ear, 'I'm going home. I have stomach ache.' She got up and left the auditorium. After a moment's thought – he was enjoying the film even though it was the tenth time – Glebov went out after her. He wasn't quite sure why he had followed her; they both felt embarrassed and neither of them spoke. Dina walked fast, almost at a run, and Glebov kept pace alongside her. In silence they crossed the street and emerged onto the Kanava Embankment. The water under the bridge was black and smoking with wisps of vapour. Here and there ice floes were still floating down the river. It was April and impossible to tell exactly whether it was warm or cold, but Glebov's teeth were chattering slightly and he was somehow shivering all over. He was now longing for Dina to kiss him, but he could not imagine how to remind her about it. After all, he hadn't missed half the film and followed her out for nothing. In fact, it had worked out very well, because Walrus and Chemist had stayed in the cinema; otherwise the four of them would have had to go home together. That would have been awkward.

Glancing sideways at Dina Lampshade, he saw her crimson cheek, her snub nose, her black hair curling out from under her woollen ski cap. He noticed that she seemed to be puffing from walking so fast. Her thick lips were parted, and the sight gave him pleasure – because he felt that Dina Lampshade, fat and not very pretty though she might be, was at that moment in his power. And she herself had agreed to it. His heart was thumping. he clenched his fists. Suddenly Dina slowed down, and Glebov, too, slackened his pace. They were passing an old four-storey house, but it was not her home: she lived on the Polyanka. Dina opened the heavy front door, went inside without looking round, and Glebov went in after her. She ran up the stairs to the first floor, onward up to the second and third, with Glebov close behind. From the third floor a small narrow staircase led higher, and Dina climbed up it. Glebov followed her. At the top was a low, dark, smelly little landing in front of a small door leading to the attic.

Breathing hard, Dina turned to him and said, 'All right.'

'What?' he asked, panting.

'You may kiss me.'

'Why do *I* have to kiss *you?* You promised . . .'

'You fool!' said Dina.

They stood in silence, growing a little calmer as they got their breath back. She refused to go away and said softly. 'Oh, you're such a fool.'

He had firmly decided to wait until she kept her promise. About three minutes passed in complete silence and immobility, and then an ear-splitting cat's screech came from behind the door leading to the attic and something furry shot past them in headlong flight. They burst out laughing, and suddenly Dina brought her hot, fat face close to his and he felt the touch – lasting for one second – of something damp around his lips, and that was the first kiss of his life. He felt no particular pleasure, merely relief. They ran back down the stairs and parted at the front door: she had to go to the right and around the corner to the Polyanka, while he ran home across the bridge.

A day or two later, at the height of Glebov's supremacy, came his downfall. Shulepnikov invited several of his schoolmates to his home after school. Glebov had been in the big house before: he had occasionally visited Walrus on the ninth floor, where the windows looked out over the Crimean Bridge and the trees of Gorky Park; in summer you could see the park's huge Ferris wheel turning round. At other times he had visited Chemist, who lived on the floor below and had fixed up a signalling system with Walrus consisting of flags on a piece of string between their balconies; he had also been to see Sonya Ganchuk and Anton's little flat on the ground floor, where he lived with his mother, Anna Georgievna. Of all the inhabitants of the big house, Anton Ovchinnikov was the one whom Glebov really liked. He regarded Anton as quite simply a genius – as indeed did many others. Anton was a musician, an admirer of Verdi; he could sing the whole of *Aïda* from beginning to end. Apart from that, he was the best artist in the school, with a remarkable gift for painting water colours of historic buildings and drawing profiles in Indian ink. He also wrote fantastic science-fiction novels concerned with the study of caves and archaeological remains, while he was also interested in palaeontology, oceanography, geography and mineralogy. Glebov was attracted to Anton not only because of his abilities, but because he was modest; he never bragged, he wasn't a know-all – unlike the other inhabitants Glebov knew of the big house, every one of whom showed, in however small a degree, a certain arrogance that he found obnoxious. Anton, by contrast, lived unpretentiously in a one-room flat, furnished with plain government-issue furniture; he owned no German shoes, no Finnish woollen sweaters, no flashy knives in leather sheaths and he never, as some did, brought to school carefully wrapped ham or cheese sandwiches whose aroma wafted around the whole classroom.

Glebov never particularly liked going to visit kids who lived in the big house – or to be more exact, he didn't dislike going there, but he also felt slightly wary because the lift operators would always look at him suspiciously and ask whom he was going to see. You had to give the name and the flat number, and sometimes the lift man would ring up the flat and check whether So-and-So was expected. It was unpleasant to have to stand and wait while being checked. As he talked on the house telephone, the lift operator would watch him with a penetrating stare, as though afraid that Glebov might slip into the lift and go up without permission, and this made Glebov feel almost like a criminal caught red-handed. And one never knew what the people up in the flat might say in reply: in Walrus's home there was a deaf maid who could never understand or explain anything properly, while in Chemist's flat the telephone was often picked up by his grandmother, a nasty old woman who kept an ever-vigilant eye on her grandson and all his doings. One day she said to the lift man that he was not to let young Glebov come up, because Chemist hadn't finished his homework. It was only when Glebov visited Anton that he was spared the agony of being interrogated and cross-questioned, because Anton's flat was on the ground floor and the most that the lift operator could do was to watch with stern attention as Glebov rang the bell and the door was opened to let him in. Glebov noticed, too, that even the kids who lived there were scared of the lift men and tried to sneak past them.

Lev Shulepnikov, however, although he had only recently come to live there, behaved differently. The lift operator, a gloomy, bespectacled man with pendulous cheeks, would first greet Shulepa with a nod and make a little movement as if to stand up behind his large desk, while Shulepa would walk past without paying him any attention. The lift would hold only five people, and even then the doors were barely able to shut. Once the lift man tried to stop Lev and his friends but timidly, trying to make a joke of it: 'Hey, you won't get stuck between floors, will you?' Boldly, Lev answered 'Who cares? Shall we risk it?' And everyone, of course, shouted in chorus: 'Let's risk it! An experiment! Let's check the lifting capacity.' And as the lift rose, the bespectacled man's face froze in a look of fear.

In the flat, whose gigantic dimensions always amazed Glebov – the passages and rooms reminded him of a museum – the mood of tomfoolery had continued. They took off their shoes and slid in their socks over the highly polished parquet floors, falling over, bumping into each other, and roaring with laughter. Suddenly from out of a white door with purple frosted-glass panels there appeared an old woman with a cigarette in her mouth who said: 'What is all this hooliganism? Stop it at once! Put your shoes on and go straight to the nursery.' Lev obeyed, grumbling, and the others followed asking him, 'Who's that? Is she your mother?' He said it was Agnes, a woman who taught French to his aunt and told tales on him to his mother. 'One day I'll poison her with arsenic. Or I'll rape her.'

Everyone burst out laughing, although at the same time they were shocked and amazed: the things Lev said! None of them would have dared to say the word 'rape' aloud; they all knew what it meant, and although they often uttered much more indecent words without a twinge of conscience, the startling thing was the casual, free-and-easy way that Lev used the word in relation to himself and the old hag with the cigarette in her mouth. And the more clearly Glebov perceived the special qualities that distinguished Lev Shulepnikov, the heavier grew that 'agony from the unfairness of things' in Glebov's heart until it eventually turned to lead. Ever since those crazy years Shulepnikov had acquired such a habit of using that word absolutely pointlessly, simply as an empty threat or a cheap joke, that he went on repeating it in later life, when he was already grown up and a post-graduate student: 'If she doesn't give me at least a 'B', I'll *rape* her.'

Back then in the nursery, furnished with strange bamboo furniture, with carpets on the floor, with bicycle wheels and boxing gloves hanging on the wall, with an enormous glass globe that revolved when the lamp inside it was switched on, and with an old-fashioned telescope on the window ledge, firmly fitted on a tripod for ease of observation – Lev said it was fun to pass the time in the evenings looking into the windows on the other side of the courtyard – it was in that room that Glebov's fragile power was destroyed. Lev brought out a film projector, hung a sheet on the wall and showed a film. It was *The Blue Express*. The projector rattled, the film kept breaking, the titles flickered past illegibly; even so, everyone was thrilled, and Glebov suddenly felt deeply hurt and offended. He thought: 'Why the hell should one person have everything, absolutely everything? Even the one thing that someone else has, which he can be a little proud of and make use of, is taken away from him and given to another who already has everything.' In time, he came to terms with it. People who can't change things come to terms with them.

Glebov got used to the big house, which kept his street in the shade in the morning; he got used to its hallways, to its lift men, to the fact that he was invited to drink tea and that Alina Fyodorovna, Lev's mother, could prod a slice of cake with a fork and push it away, saying, 'This cake is stale' – and the cake was removed. When this happened for the first time, Glebov was secretly amazed. How could a cake be stale? It struck him as an absolutely stupid idea. Cake was a rarity at home; it appeared only on somebody's birthday, it was

21

quickly eaten, and it never occurred to anyone to say whether it was fresh or stale, because it was always fresh, deliciously fresh, especially the gorgeous kind decorated with roses made of pink icing!

Glebov also came to terms with his own flat. After a visit to the big house he at first used to feel somehow depressed whenever he suddenly saw, as if he were a stranger, his little lopsided house with its yellowish-brown coating of stucco; whenever he climbed the dark staircase, where you had to go carefully because the steps were broken in places; whenever he approached the front door, dotted with nameplates, inscriptions and bells like an old patched blanket; whenever he plunged into the many-layered, paraffin-smelling atmosphere of the building, where something was always bubbling in a saucepan and someone was always boiling cabbage; whenever he washed his hands in the bathroom, where movement was difficult because of all the planks that covered the bathtub, in which no one ever took a bath or washed laundry, but which was covered with the bowls and washbasins belonging to the various tenants of the flat; whenever he saw, felt and noticed much else besides on returning from Lev Shulepnikov's or someone else's in the big house: but gradually it all subsided, softened, and ceased to upset him.

One day, after a visit to Lev, he was excitedly describing the chandelier in the dining room of the Shulepnikovs' flat, the hallway that was so long you could ride a bike in it, the sweets that were served at tea – it wasn't the sweets that amazed him but the size of the box they were in – and his mother and grandmother were questioning him with great curiosity about this, that and the other in Lev's home, when his father suddenly winked at Glebov and said:

'Just listen to them – sounds to me as if they'd like to live in that house. Would you?'

'Well, why not?' said his mother. 'I'd like to have my own hallway too.'

'And I'd like to live somewhere where people don't rattle crockery,' said Nila, Glebov's grandmother. Their next-door neighbour used to come home from work late and at midnight would start shuffling back and forth between her room and the communal kitchen, always for some reason carrying crockery that rattled. Old Nila slept on top of a large trunk by the door, and the neighbour's rattling crockery used to wake her up. Father looked pityingly at mother and grandmother.

'What am I to do with you? You're like a couple of old hens clucking away in a barnyard . . .'

He was always making harmless little jokes like that – his pet name for his wife was 'my speckled hen'. The women would pretend to be indignant and would go for him, waving their arms, but mother never really lost her temper with anybody, and father would nudge Glebov and wink.

'Did you ever see such silly hens?' he said now. 'Don't you two realise that if you don't have a hallway in your flat there's all the more space for the other rooms?' And as for rattling crockery – why, it's music. I wouldn't move into the big house if you gave me two thousand roubles . . .'

Although his father almost always seemed to be half-joking and flippant and constantly teased mother, grandmother and mother's sister, Aunt Paula, with practical jokes that would give them a fright (at times it was hard to tell whether he was really acting in fun), in reality – it was not until Glebov was almost grown up that he realised this – he was not at all flippant by nature and not really a cheerful person either. It was all an act, put on for the family. Deep inside his father's personality, like a hidden core around which all the rest of him was wound, was a significant quality – caution. The phrase that he often spoke, laughingly – 'Now my children, obey the sign in the tramcars: Don't stick your head out!' – was not just a bit of fun. It was a wise maxim, which, diffidently and as though unintentionally, he was always trying to instill in the family. But *why* shouldn't one stick one's head out? He apparently regarded this rule as so important, the sense of it so self-evident, that it needed no explanation. He seemed to feel suffocated, as though by some ancient traumatic fear. He was much older tha his wife; with his curly grey hair he looked like an old man, although he was only fifty, but those had been fifty years of struggle, adversity and hard knocks. He had come from the very poor family of a clerk, who had worked at the Dux factory. His father's brother, Uncle Nikolai, had been an aviator, one of the first Russian pilots to be shot down and killed in the war against Germany. The family was very proud of him. They had nothing else to be proud of. The portrait of Uncle Nikolai in his school cap hung in a prominent place. Even Glebov's friendship with Lev Shulepnikov – for some incomprehensible reason Lev liked Glebov; he often invited him home and gave him books (he seemed indifferent about books in general, and Glebov harboured the suspicion that he pinched them from his father's library, because some of them bore a blue stamp showing a man with a hammer, the rays of the sun and the inscription 'Ex libris A.V.S.') – even in this childish friendship Glebov's father perceived some danger and advised him 'not to stick his head out'. He suggested that Glebov go less often to the big house and not to be flattered by Lev's friendship because 'the Shulepnikovs have their place in life, you have yours, and you shouldn't try and mix them'.

For some reason his father always seemed to think Glebov would soon start to bore Lev Shulepnikov, or worse still, Lev's parents, and that this might cause unpleasantness. Deep inside, Glebov himself sensed this, too; somehow he didn't really *want* to spend time in the big house; yet he went there whenever he was invited, and sometimes even without an invitation. The place was tempting because it was so unusual – the things he and Anton talked about, the books Sonya Ganchuk showed him from her father's library, the marvels that Shulepa used to brag about. At home, on the other hand, everything was deadeningly familiar, everything was dull and tedious.

His father rarely said anything directly – it was usually implied in hints and little jokes. Glebov, though, insisted on making him spell out his feelings about Lev. 'Why do you talk like that about him? Why do you think Lev isn't good for me?'

His father never fathomed the real reason why Lev wasn't 'good' for Glebov, or rather the thing that provoked that horrible, leaden, sinking feeling inside him. His father had other considerations in mind; but he always avoided explaining what they were, or he would say something absurd, such as: 'In principle I have nothing against Lev, or Shulepa, as you call him . . . By the way, I'd advise you not to use that nickname. Just call him Lev . . . The fact is that he is badly brought up. For instance, he never says "thank you" when he gets up from the tea table.'

This was, of course, nonsense; his father was just being evasive. He disliked Lev for some other, some more significant reason. Yet whenever Lev came to visit, his father always welcomed him, even treated him kindly and courteously as though he were a grown-up; he would make a point of calling him 'Lev', which Glebov thought very funny. Apart from that, in Lev's presence his father always became unusually talkative and discussed all sorts of things with him, and became – to Glebov's embarrassment – prone to boast and exaggerate.

One day, when talking about Uncle Nikolai, he announced that his brother had been the first Russian pilot to shoot down three enemy aeroplanes in one dogfight, including the plane flown by the famous German air ace Count von Schwerin. The count's plane had crashed, but by a miracle the count himself survived and was soon flying again, having announced that his one ambition was to meet that Russian again in a dogfight and have his revenge. The story had been published in all the newspapers.

Glebov listened, squirming with embarrassment. His father said to him, 'Even you don't know about this. I've never told you before.'

Lev Shulepnikov said, 'Last time you told me about it, you said he had shot down two aeroplanes.'

'I did? Impossible. I couldn't have said it was two, because that wouldn't have been a record. Two wasn't a record. The whole point was that he shot down *three* enemy planes in one dogfight.'

Another time his father had described how, during the Civil War, he himself had served in the Caucasus under the command of Comrade Kirov (it was true that he had indeed served some time in the Caucasus) and how he had even been with a cavalry detachment in Persia, where he had seen fire worshippers. Lev Shulepnikov immediately topped this with an invented story about his father, who, he claimed, had personally shot a fakir in Tiflis. Glebov's father then said that in northern India he had seen a fakir who had made a magic tree grow to full size before his very eyes. (His father had never been in northern India – that Glebov knew for sure.) Not to be outdone, Lev said that his father had once captured a gang of fakirs, imprisoned them in a cellar, and was going to shoot them as British spies, but that when he went into the cellar the next morning, there was no one there – only five frogs. And there had been five fakirs.

'He should have shot the frogs,' said Glebov's father.

'He did,' said Lev. 'But have you any idea how hard it is to shoot frogs? Especially in a cellar!'

Glebov's father laughed, wagging his finger in a mock threat that also expressed approval.

'I see, Lev, that you have a lively imagination. That's good, I like that. But joking aside, I really have seen live fakirs. Firstly in northern India, as I've said, and secondly here in Moscow, on Strastnoi Boulevard . . .'

There was a certain similarity to the senior Glebov and Lev Shulepnikov – that was why conversation between them flowed so smoothly and enjoyably. This annoyed Glebov. He was irritated by made-up stories that were passed off as truth, though not because his father exaggerated but because he said one thing behind Lev's back and something else to his face. He said to his father:

'But you said you didn't like Lev. So why do you behave like that? You smile and tell him funny stories – just as if he were your boss . . .'

At this his father lost his temper. He hardly ever got angry or shouted, but now he began shouting at Glebov: 'At your age! You dare to lecture me, you cheeky young puppy!' ('Cheeky young puppy' was one of his favourite expressions.) 'I smile and tell stories because I was taught good manners. All you young hooligans can ever do is bellow: "Hey, Lev! Hey you! Wanna fight?" What incredible cheek, to lecture your own father on how to behave.'

He got so steamed up that he complained to Glebov's mother and grandma, and they joined in the scolding. That evening, however, Glebov overheard his mother and father whispering behind the screen: 'Why do you have to talk such nonsense in front of that brat from the big house? It upsets Vadim.'

'He's too cheeky. Trying to teach his father.'

'Well, you shouldn't show his friend such deference.'

'You're all fools! You don't understand.'

A day or two later, when he had finally cooled off, Glebov's father calmly had it out with him: 'By the way, about the remark you made to me the other day . . . when you implied that I treated your young Lev as though he were an important person. It was quite sharp of you to notice. He really is – well, if not Lev, let's say his parents are *personages* of some importance, although you must never say I said so, because everything around us is all mixed up, tied together with invisible links . . .'

It was not long before this was confirmed: one thing really was tied up with another. Suddenly one day Uncle Volodya, Aunt Paula's husband, was in some sort of trouble. The family began wondering whether they might not be able to help him through Shulepnikov, Lev's father. Uncle Volodya and Aunt Paula lived nearby on the Yakimanka, but they used to pop in and out practically every day, especially Aunt Paula. Glebov's mother and grandmother were very fond of her. She was regarded as the most beautiful, the most successful member of the family, with a very good job as a designer and modeller in a toy factory. And Uncle Volodya was a typesetter in a printing shop. Some unpleasantness blew up around him, and he was practically accused of sabotage. Aunt Paula wept: 'God, how could Volodya ever be a saboteur? What harm has he ever done anyone? The only person he has ever harmed is himself.' He did himself a great deal of harm, in fact, because he was a heavy drinker. Glebov's father constantly reproached him. Mother and Grandmother alternately pitied Aunt Paula and scolded her:

'It's your own fault for letting him get in such a state. Why do you buy drink for him?'

'Well, I'd rather he got drunk at home,' was Aunt Paula's excuse, 'than in the street with his cronies.'

Grandma Nila and Glebov's mother insisted that Uncle Volodya's trouble was all due to drink, but Aunt Paula would not agree: 'It's other people who have done him in. He's just that kind of person.'

It was true that Uncle Volodya was a very good, guileless and kind man, but even at his young age Glebov had come to realise that it was exactly such softhearted and guileless people who spelled trouble for everyone around them. Aunt Paula was crying, Grandma Nila was suffering in sympathy, Glebov's mother could think about nothing else, and his father swore. That spring they had planned to buy Glebov a bicycle, but now his mother said, 'There's no money to spare right now. We've got to help Paula.'

And suddenly the thought came to them: Ask Lev's father to help. At first they rejected the idea with much finger wagging. 'Keep away from him, don't get mixed up with people like that.' Now, suddenly, it was proposed to appeal to him through Lev. The reason for this was that everyone was so impressed by the business with the Bychkovs.

The Bychkovs were a noisy, cheerful family who lived in the Glebovs' building and behaved like lords. Everyone was afraid of them; they were rude and did exactly as they pleased. They would lock the kitchen in the evening and let no one else in until they were finished; even if the neighbours called in the police, it had no effect. Old man Bychkov, Semyon Gerasievich by name, worked in a tannery, where his job was to soak leather in vats of stinking liquid. He also made boots at home, the most expensive, fashionable sorts of boots, most of which he did not actually stitch himself but gave out to others to make while he procured the leather and drummed up customers.

God, the shouting that went on because the Bychkovs locked the kitchen! The neighbour who lived across the hallway and who came home late made more fuss than anyone else. Glebov's mother also got very indignant. Firstly – there was the smell; secondly – the obnoxious behaviour.

Sometimes Mother would leap out into the hallway, shouting, 'I'll get you for this! How dare you!'

Old Semyon Gerasievich would answer back, burbling away in his deep voice. Father joined unwillingly in the fray. At once the whole Bychkov clan would pour out of the 'hall' – a large room in which all six of them lived, which for some reason they had named the 'hall' – and the hum of voices became a roar, which sounded like a thunderstorm rumbling and crashing down. The chief villains were Taranka and Minka. Taranka was ten and was a junior at school; Minka was fifteen and didn't go to school anywhere, because he had twice been kept back in the third form, then expelled, after which he went somewhere as an apprentice but dropped out. He was mixed up in some shady dealings, ended up in a billiard hall in the park and probably, some thought, the gang he belonged to were pickpockets. He was the uncrowned junior king of Deryugin Street and its environs. And he was an evil king. People were afraid of meeting him in the street because everyone knew that he always carried a knife. Once he ran into the school after lessons and started demanding: 'Who was bullying Taranka yesterday? Who made a grab at him on the staircase? Was it you, you bastard?'

He already knew who it was, because Taranka had already complained to him – or had made up the story. Most people took care not to touch the scrofulous Taranka, but there were some ignorant ones of course, who hadn't heard about Minka, so when Taranka behaved in his usual impudent way, these unfortunates would box his ears or flick the side of his head with their fingers, without guessing at the appalling consequences. In front of the brick wall in the schoolyard, to which he led his victims by the ear, Minka would set up a brief, cruel kangaroo court:

'How dare you hurt my brother? What's the matter with you – bored with life?'

He publicly humiliated and crushed Yura the Bear, a strong boy who was not afraid of even sixth formers. Minka twisted his arm behind his back until he yelled with pain. Minka only twisted harder until the Bear fell to his knees, at which Minka ordered him:

'Say "Forgive me, Taras Alexeyevich, for offending you. And I'll never do it again.".'

All the while Taranka, a skinny little brat with ginger eyelashes, just stood watching and laughing. Yura stuck it out to the limit of his endurance, groaned, ground his teeth and shook his head – he didn't want to give in – but in the end Bychkov won. Taranka came up to him and shoved his foot in Yura's face, and Minka twisted his arm harder and harder:

'Come on, slob – give! Or you'll lose your arm.'

Then Yura whispered, barely audibly: 'Forgive me, Taras Alexeyevich . . .' and all the rest. No one came to Yura's rescue: there were no big boys in the yard, and the smaller ones could do nothing. Glebov was also afraid of Minka Bychkov, but not in the way the others were. Minka was, after all, a neighbour. Now and again he would ask Glebov to do him a favour, and at other times he would give him something in return. Sometimes Glebov secretly felt proud that everyone else was afraid to go down Deryugin Street because of Minka Bychkov and his gang, but he was never afraid. He would even walk along the street late in the evening or at night and no one touched him. Glebov was keenly conscious of his superiority in this respect, and he even felt – with a certain secret shame, never admitting it to himself – that if he was ever attacked Taranka and Minka would stand up for him and hit back on his behalf.

Glebov, however, never squealed to Minka about anyone, and in general he never made use of the possible sinister advantages of being under Minka's neighbourly protection, because beneath his smug sense of security, deep down there lurked another feeling – fear, which turned his heart to ice, a fear such as no one else had experienced, because no one else knew those Bychkovs quite so well, the Bychkovs whose mere voices made his mother turn pale and his grandmother cross herself.

His mother had said to him, 'For God's sake, never have anything to do with either Minka or Taranka.' But how could he help it, when they forced themselves on him? How could he keep away from them? They had a sister called Vera, a girl of sixteen, who worked in a factory. She looked absolutely like a grown-up woman – at least, so it seemed to Glebov. She was all fleshy curves, with big jutting breasts and squeaky shoes, and she always reeked of eau-de-cologne.

Taranka once enticed Glebov out in the hallway and said urgently, 'Want to see Vera naked? Gimme twenty kopecks.'

Glebov, of course, had no such desire. He was completely uninterested in looking at Vera in the nude; the mere thought of it gave him a nasty feeling. And where was he to get twenty kopecks? Pinch them from his mother or beg them from his grandmother? But Taranka was fiercely insistent and threatened him with the dog: the Bychkovs had a large black dog called Abdul, which was regarded as Minka's property. Glebov knew Abdul well, but even so, once they set the dog on him, you never knew how it might end.

They went into the bathroom, took a washbasin off the planks across the bathtub, put a stool on the planks, and Glebov climbed up on it. Up above, just below the ceiling, was a small internal window that looked into the 'hall', covered by a little curtain on the bathroom side. Taranka pulled the curtain aside and Glebov watched Vera washing herself all over in a tin tub in the middle of the room. Vera saw what was going on but for some reason was not embarrassed. Glebov saw everything.

Then Taranka sank his teeth into Glebov like a tick: 'Gimme twenty kopecks right away!' The whole family was like that – give, give, hand it over now. It happened more than once that Glebov's mother came in so flustered that she was almost in a state of panic: 'Alevtina wants to borrow my sewing machine again. What shall I say to her?'

Alevtina was the wife of the oldest Bychkov son and mother of Minka, Taranka and Vera. Mother hated lending her sewing machine to this woman. She tried her best to wriggle out of it now, but Alevtina always got what she wanted. It was impossible to escape the clutches of the Bychkovs.

Their rule came to an end in the following way. One day Lev and Anton were walking down Deryugin Street, although they were not coming to see Glebov; they were simply using the street as a shortcut that led through several backyards to the Kanava Embankment. The Bychkovs intercepted them, Taranka first taunting them with stupid remarks: 'Hey, kid, wanna ess in the kay?' which meant 'Want a sock in the kisser?' and was in effect a challenge to a fight. Naturally they paid no attention to Taranka and simply brushed him aside. This was the signal for Minka's gang to pour out of a doorway – this was their standard scenario – and start a fight. One of them let Abdul off the leash, and although he didn't actually bite anyone, he gave the victims a bad fright and tore their clothes. This didn't bother Lev too much, but to Anton every scrap of clothing was precious. The next day a man in a long leather overcoat came to Glebov's house and straightaway knocked on the door of the 'hall'. Abdul barked loudly.

Old man Bychkov, Alevtina and Taranka were at home. There was a noise, voices; Alevtina shouted and the dog barked and whined. Glebov was not allowed to go out into the hallway and the whole Glebov family sat and listened intently. Then came the sound of three revolver shots . . . Abdul, it was said later, had crawled under the divan and refused to come out.

Glebov was disappointed: he had thought the dog was brave and fierce, but it had behaved like a coward. He felt rather sorry for the Bychkovs, especially Alevtina and Taranka, although everyone else in the building rejoiced. After the destruction of Abdul, the whole Bychkov clan seemed to fall apart. Minka was arrested for complicity in a robbery, old Semyon Gerasievich fell down in the yard and was taken to hospital, and soon all the other Bychkovs vanished, no one knew where, as though they had been blown away by the wind. The 'hall' was partitioned into two rooms and decorated with new wallpaper. The new tenants, by the name of Pomrachinsky – husband, wife and daughter Lyuba – were as quiet and unobtrusive as mice and always talked to one another in whispers.

I still remember all those trifles of childhood, the losses and the finds; how he made me suffer when he wouldn't wait for me and went to school with someone else; how the building where the chemist's was, was moved – complete – to another site; how the air in the backyards was always damp, smelling of the river, and how the smell of the river penetrated into our rooms, especially my father's big room, and how when a tram crossed the bridge the metallic clatter and squeak of its wheels could be heard from far away. I remember running in one breath all the way up the huge flight of stone steps at the side of the bridge; in the evening, running into the Deryugin Street gang under the archway as they came tumbling out of the cinema like a pack of hyenas – and walking towards them, fists clenched, petrified with fear.

The whole of our childhood was enveloped in a crimson cloud of vanity.

Oh, those exertions, that striving, that thirst for a moment of glory! The world was small, made up of five or six others – Anton, Chemist, Walrus, perhaps Sonya and Lev too, and of course Yarik, the class clown – and our little universe seethed with a longing to do one thing: prove ourselves. Tender, juicy, scarlet flesh of childhood. Everything was unique, incomparable: the first time I ran out onto the embankment during breaktime, onto the sun-soaked asphalt; the first time I realised that spring simply meant a cold wind that made your teeth chatter. A thin, stooping man in a short overcoat, wearing a large brick-red woman's beret on his head, was walking rapidly along the pavement and talking to himself. Some insane preoccupation devoured his sunken cheeks and deep-set eyes. Reading the name of our school as he passed by, he suddenly stopped and shouted, 'It can't be! It doesn't exist in nature. Do you hear?' He was not shouting at us, a frightened bunch of kids huddling beside the parapet of the embankment, but to some invisible person who had inflamed his hatred. ' "B.O.S.O.M. High School." What bosom?

32

What is this crap? My God, do they know what they're doing?'

Eyes flashing, he uttered a few more angry imprecations, then suddenly leaped up onto the narrow granite coping of the parapet and walked several paces along it with as much ease and unconcern as if he had been walking along the pavement. The boys froze; the girls shrieked in horror. The man in the beret seemed to notice them for the first time; he stopped, stared down at them from above and said, 'Unfortunate children!'

After which, he ran for several yards along the parapet with a lunatic gait, jumped down and hurried away in the direction of the Moskvoretsky Bridge. It was my first encounter with a madman. This man stunned us all. When he was a safe distance away, we began laughing crazily. Chemist went up to the parapet and climbed onto it, hauling himself up with his hands. We could see that he was afraid and could hardly bring himself to straighten up; yet he was the first to stand up on the parapet. Then he pulled an agonised face, waved his arms and shouted, 'Unfortunate children!' – and collapsed on to the pavement like an old sack. We laughed – until Anton Ovchinnikov, pale as death, lips pressed tightly together, strode up to the parapet and also climbed onto it, straightened up and put out his arms like a tightrope walker. We knew that Anton had flat feet, that he was short-sighted and subject to epileptic fits, but no one stopped him. We were all overcome by a sort of madness. It appeared that to walk, even to run along the parapet was incredibly easy. After Anton, the ponderous fat boy known as Walrus climbed up and shuffled along the granite coping-stone without lifting the soles of his shoes; crouching like a monkey, but when he jumped down onto the pavement, his legs gave way under him and he fell to his knees. Then I climbed up, then Yarik.

It wasn't all that difficult; the trick was not to think about anything but to keep looking at the granite pathway under your feet. A fearful shriek from one of the teachers wrenched us out of our strange trance. It was probably that shriek that saved Yarik, who was the clumsiest and most helpless of all of us; he couldn't run, couldn't wrestle, couldn't hold his own in the school yard, the scene of fist-fights in which the first to draw blood was the winner. Yarik was red-haired, white-faced and somehow totally soft, like a rubber toy. He reminded one of a bird that couldn't fly. He was bullied by boys from other forms who were always on the lookout for someone to beat up. He was a tempting prey: so big and so boneless. Once even a junior beat him up. The whole trouble was that Yarik was simply incapable of hitting anyone: his fingers would not clench into a fist, and so he never resisted when anyone went for him, even little kids. We always defended Yarik, and sometimes pitched battles would develop from our attempts to save him; he was, after all, the property of our form, and anyone who raised a hand against him was insulting us all. Suddenly there would come a shout: 'Yarik's in trouble!' – and we would gallop headlong up to the first or second floor, to the gymnasium or into the yard, wherever the villains were giving our Yarik a rough time: they would crowd him into a corner and punch him up or make him give some big fat lout a piggy-back ride. But that time on the embankment, as he approached the parapet and with a desperate look bent his long, stilt-like legs to jump up, we all stared at Yarik with delighted interest, expecting an entertaining spectacle. In fact, if that teacher hadn't shrieked, he would almost certainly have fallen into the water and drowned.

That was how it all began – testing our nerve. After we had learned not only to walk but to run along the top of the parapet – almost all of our gang, except Yarik and a boy who had one crippled leg (he was permanently excused from P.T.) – Anton dreamed up another ordeal: walking down Deryugin Street at night. The nastiest district on the island, and probably in the whole of left-bank Moscow, it was a haunt of the shadiest characters: muggers and robbers to whom nothing was sacred; bandits who attacked merchants' wagons, privateers and pirate crews like those led by the one-legged Long John Silver. Any kid who ventured into the street was unscrupulously robbed: one would lose a ten-kopeck piece, another fifteen kopecks, while others were relieved of a penknife or fountain pen. Parents forbade their children to go there.

But did we ever get our own back if any of them were rash enough to stray into *our* yards?

Anton practised jujitsu. As an exercise – at break, in lessons, at home, reading a book or listening to music on the radio – from morning till night he would hit the outer edge of his right hand against some hard object. This was supposed to make the hand as hard as iron. He called it 'armouring' his hand, and as in everything that Anton did, thanks to his almost inhuman persistence and self-discipline, the 'armouring' technique proved successful. After about two months, his hand had become embellished with a thick, hard callous. None of us others would have had the patience to achieve this. So when the Deryugin Street gang jumped out of a doorway and barred our way and Minka Bychkov – big and tough and already sprouting a moustache – asked, 'What are you doing here? Are you coming to see Vadim Glebov?' Anton answered, 'No!' Anton and Lev did sometimes go and visit Glebov; they thought he was OK and not too much of a crap-eater. Most of the kids in our class were, of course, crap-eaters. But on this occasion Anton firmly said, 'No!' although if he had said they were going to Vadim's, the gang wouldn't have touched us. If we had shouted, 'Hey! French Loaf!' (Vadim Glebov's nickname was 'French Loaf') and Vadim had looked out of the window, there might have been no fight.

Anton, however, had set up the whole escapade to test our nerve, and we were not supposed to lighten the ordeal in any way. Lev Shulepnikov had purposely left his blank-cartridge pistol at home. Poor Anton Ovchinnikov certainly didn't look like a hero or an athlete – later, after the fight, legends about him sprang up around all the neighbouring backyards – but he was short and stocky, one of the shortest boys in the class; he always wore shorts right into the coldest part of the winter as a way of physically hardening himself, and this made him look excessively young and childish. People who didn't know him never took him seriously. To top it all, he wore glasses whenever he went to the cinema or travelled out of town. He was, it seems, wearing his glasses then, in Deryugin Street. So when the gang lazily closed in on us – one of us was tripped up, another was jostled, somebody tried to snatch Anton's glasses off his nose – suddenly something happened that was like a bomb exploding: Anton hit his attacker in the pit of the stomach with the edge of his hand, and the lout collapsed. He hit another, who also fell down; then he lashed out at a third . . . They fell instantly, without shouting, without struggling, as though of their own volition, like well-trained clowns falling onto a mat in the circus ring. Those were fabulous moments. Then they beat us up horribly, and there was that dog . . . Anton was in bed at home for a month with a bandaged head, but somehow we rejoiced immeasurably at the whole affair. Yet what did we have to be pleased about? It seems so strange and inexplicable now. We visited Anton in his rather dark little flat on the ground floor, where the sun never penetrated, where beside the portraits of composers there hung his water colours, in shades of yellow and blue, where a young, clean-shaven man with officer's insignia looked at us from a photograph in a heavy wooden frame on the piano – Anton's father had died in Central Asia, killed by the *basmachi* rebels; where the radio was always on; where in a secret drawer of his desk lay a stack of thick fifty-five-kopeck school notebooks, every page covered with tiny handwriting; where cockroaches rustled over sheets of newspaper in the bathroom (there were cockroaches in all the bathrooms in that section of the building); where we all sat in the kitchen and ate cold potatoes, sprinkling them with salt, in between bites of big slices of delicious black bread; where we laughed, fantasised, reminisced, dreamed and rejoiced – God knows why – like fools.

Again the talk turned to Uncle Volodya: could he be helped through Lev Shulepnikov's father? It now appeared that the latter was a powerful man. It was Glebov's mother who raised the subject. His father hesitated. 'You shouldn't bother people,' he said, obviously extremely nervous. 'It's a trivial matter to a man like Shulepnikov; it's embarrassing to ask.' Mother said, 'You never liked Volodya. But he's my brother. And I feel sorry for Paula and the children. No, I shall definitely ask Lev to speak to his father.'

'I forbid you to do that!' shouted Glebov's father.

Glebov's mother rarely argued with his father, but she usually did what she wanted anyway. One evening Lev Shulepnikov came to visit – Glebov was helping him with his algebra, and in any case he just liked to drop in and chat – and they were sitting down to tea and buttered rolls; Lev liked drinking tea with the Glebovs, complaining that they never had rolls at home. Suddenly Glebov's mother again raised the subject of Uncle Volodya, asking whether someone could find out about it and help, because there had obviously been a misunderstanding. Lev agreed casually: 'All right, I'll tell my dad.' Mother handed him a piece of paper with Uncle Volodya's full name, which she had written out in advance. Glebov could almost physically feel his father go tense and contract his muscles; he was stirring the sugar in his tea glass at that moment and suddenly the movement of his hand and the tinkling of the spoon stopped, and he froze, motionless, without lifting his head. But Glebov's mother was smiling, her eyes glistening, and when she drew close to him Glebov realised that her breath smelled of liquor. He wasn't very pleased with his mother's initiative either, because Shulepa was after all *his* friend and if he had to be asked about something then he, Glebov, should have done it.

When Lev had gone, Glebov's father bombarded his mother with reproaches: 'Aren't you ashamed of yourself? You're drunk! You talk to our guest in a state of intoxication.' Mother, of course, denied that she was drunk and told him not to talk nonsense. In fact she was not drunk; she had simply taken a nip or two for Dutch courage. Glebov's father flew into a temper, shouting that he wouldn't answer for his actions, that he declined all responsibility: the exact nature of his threat was not very clear. He was generally rather fond of uttering obscure threats. Glebov had rarely seen his father so upset. He even banged his fist on the table and shouted in confused anger: 'I do everything for you! Every step! And you – what the hell do you do? Chicken-brains!' Only later did Glebov realise that his father was frightened to death. He also had another characteristic: he only got angry about things that he refused to talk about aloud. One had to guess what the real reason was; this was difficult to do, at times impossible. But when he caught Mother with a glass of vodka, which she was surreptitiously drinking in a little bar on the Polyanka, the reason for his anger was clear: the conversation about Uncle Volodya. He had categorically forbidden it, and Glebov's mother had disobeyed him.

Only when he had finally finished blowing his top and had shouted himself hoarse, did he say, apparently casually: 'And as for that stupid business about Volodya . . . How could you bring yourself to say it?' Glebov's mother burst into tears and his father angrily stamped out of the room, slamming the door. But his grandmother said calmly to Glebov, 'Dima, you must remind your friend Lev about it. Don't mind all the fuss. We've got to help him.'

Grandma Nila had a gift of always quietly saying something simple and sensible when everyone else around was losing his head and shouting nonsense. Glebov loved this bent little old lady with her grey hair still faintly streaked with pale blonde, a neat bun on the back of her head, and a tiny little yellowish face. She was forever pattering about the house, doing chores and scurrying here and there. In fact, she bore the whole household on her back, and was on her feet from early morning till late at night. And she alone, it seemed to Glebov, *sometimes* understood him.

One frosty day Glebov was sitting in Lev's room playing chess when Lev's father suddenly came in. It was their third game, and they were playing 'best of three'. Glebov hardly ever saw Shulepnikov senior – perhaps three or four times in his whole life. Lev used to say that his father worked round the clock; he was hardly ever at home and even slept at work. Lev called him 'dad', although in fact he was Lev's stepfather; his real father, who had a strange double-barrelled surname, had died or disappeared in some mysterious fashion from Lev's life. Prokhorov-Pluhnge. That was Lev's father's name, and twenty years later Lev himself reverted to his real name: Prokhorov, but without the Pluhnge. But that was in quite a different life. Besides Shulepnikov and the vanished Prokhorov-Pluhnge, there was a third father, whose name was Fiveisky or Flavitsky. It was easy to get confused between Lev's fathers, but his mother always remained one and the same. She was a remarkable woman; Lev used to say that she came from a noble family and that through her he was a descendant of the princes Baryatinsky.

Alina Fyodorovna, Lev's mother, was a dark, olive-complexioned woman with a stern voice and a proud bearing. Glebov had the impression that she was the real head of the family and Lev was more afraid of her than of his stepfather. She was something in between the indomitable Boyarina Morozova in Surikov's picture and the old countess in Pushkin's *The Queen of Spades*. Shulepnikov himself, Lev's stepfather, was a short, unprepossessing man with slightly protuberant eyes, who spoke in a quiet voice; his face astonished Glebov by its almost absolute bloodlessness. Glebov had never seen such pallid, immobile features in any other human being. Lev's stepfather wore a grey military tunic belted in by a thin, silver-buckled Caucasian strap, grey breeches and boots. He came into the room, watched the chess game for a short while and asked:

'Vadim Glebov – that's you, isn't it?'

Glebov nodded.

'Come with me for a minute.'

Glebov hesitated. He didn't want to abandon the game in a winning situation, when he was two knights ahead of Lev.

'That's it! A draw!' shouted Lev, and swept the pieces off the board. Dispirited, thinking how low-down and unfair Shulepa was, Glebov followed Lev's stepfather into his study. He had no inkling of what he was about to hear.

'Sit down.'

Glebov sat down in a dark cherry-red leather armchair, which was so soft that it was like falling down a hole, and he felt slightly alarmed, but quickly recovered his composure and found a comfortable, relaxed position. Lev's stepfather said: 'Lev has given me a note from your mother about . . .' He put on his spectacles and read out: '. . . Vladimir Grigorievich Burmistrov. He's a relation of yours, isn't he? Very well, I'll try and find out some information about his case, if that's possible. If not, please don't blame me. But I have a favour to ask you, too, Vadim.'

Sitting behind a vast desk, Shulepnikov senior looked so small and downcast, his shoulders slumped with exhaustion, doodling on a sheet of paper.

'Tell me, Vadim, who was the ringleader of that gangster-like attack on my son Lev in the school yard?'

Glebov was stupefied. He never expected to be asked any such question. He thought that affair was long since forgotten – after all, it had happened several months ago. He too had been one of the ringleaders, although he had ducked out at the last moment. But it was always possible that someone had told this about him. All this instantly passed through Glebov's mind and he began to get cold feet. Seeing that Glebov was reduced to embarrased silence, Shulepnikov said sternly, 'Attacking my son is not a trivial matter. It was done by a group, but there must have been ringleaders who organised it. Who were they?'

Glebov mumbled that he didn't know. He felt extremely uncomfortable – so much so that he began to feel a gnawing pain in the pit of his stomach. Lev's stepfather didn't seem to be a man given to anger; he didn't shout or swear, but in his low voice and the look in his bright, slightly bulging eyes there was something that made it uncomfortable to sit opposite him in a soft armchair. Glebov was convinced that there was no way out of this situation and he would have to own up. Perhaps the fate of Uncle Volodya depended on this. He began by trying to mislead, by talking about Minka and Taranka, but Lev's stepfather brusquely cut him short, saying that business was over and no longer of any interest. Who was the ringleader of the attack in the school yard? So far these boys had not been discovered and had not been punished. Agonised, Glebov hesitated, lacking the courage to open his mouth, and they sat like this in silence for some time until the unforeseen happened: a loud and very obvious rumbling came from his stomach. It was so unexpected and so shameful that Glebov shrank, pulled his head down between his shoulders and froze into horrified immobility. The rumbling would not stop, but Lev's stepfather paid no attention to it. He said:

'You see, Lev has a great failing – he is obstinate. He has dug his heels in and refuses to testify out of a false sense of comradeship. You know, I expect, that he is not my own son – he is Alina Fyodorovna's son – and that complicates the matter, because I am unable to, shall we say, exert any pressure on him. What am I to do? You must help me, Vadim. You're twelve years old, you're a big boy now and you know how serious this is. It is very, very serious.' And he raised a warning finger.

The rumbling in his stomach had stopped, but Glebov was afraid that it would start up again at any moment. Prompted by this fear, he told his tale: he named the boy called Yura the Bear, who really had been the chief instigator and whom Glebov disliked because he sometimes used to take advantage of his strength to give someone an unprovoked rabbit punch, and he named Manyunya, who was notoriously grasping and selfish. He told himself this was quite fair, because those who would be punished were bad. Yet even though he had done no more than tell the plain truth about two bad boys, he had an uncomfortable feeling of having betrayed them – and that feeling stayed with Glebov for a long time, probably for several days.

Later, Lev came to see Glebov to say that his father had been unable to find out anything about Uncle Volodya. No one was particularly annoyed or disappointed, because they had already guessed that nothing would come of it. Uncle Volodya was already in a prison camp in the north and had written a letter home. Nor did anything very terrible happen to the Bear or Manyunya either. The Bear's parents changed jobs and left Moscow, taking their son with them, and Manyunya got such bad marks that he was expelled from school; he was sent to a reform school, from which he ran away, got mixed up with a bunch of crooks and spent the war years in a prison camp. There was one more incident: that spring, soon after Manyunya's expulsion from school he came to the courtyard of the big house, lay in wait for Lev and roughed him up. The rumour went around that this was because of some girl, but Glebov knew what it was really about.

It is all so long ago now, it has all become so blurred and distorted, fallen apart like a piece of old, rotten fabric that it is hard to remember what really happened. Why did this happen, why that? Why did he act like that and no differently? Only trivia survive, fixed in the memory: they are imperishable, immortal. The rumbling in his stomach, for instance. And what was it that stuck in his memory several years afterwards, when fate again brought him together with Lev Shulepnikov in the institute and when Sonya and her father Professor Ganchuk crossed his path once more? Again, trivia: the sight of Professor Ganchuk greedily eating a Napoleon cake in a café on Gorky Street after the meeting at which he was destroyed. Glebov had happened to pass by and had seen him through the window.

In the autumn of 1947, when Glebov caught sight of Lev Shulepnikov in the courtyard of the institute and recognised him, despite the fact that in the intervening seven years Lev had become a different person – tall, with a prominent forehead and the beginnings of premature baldness, wearing a little dark red Caucasian-style moustache, which was not merely a fashion of the time but indicated character, life-style and even ideological outlook – apart from amazement and curiosity, in the very first second Glebov felt a stab of that forgotten, *leaden* feeling that was forever linked with Shulepnikov. They roared with laughter, punched and pulled at each other, bellowing cheerfully: 'Who's that?' 'Who's that character over there?' 'What's that guy doing here?' – yet at the same time Glebov felt the familiar depression weighing on him. In his out-at-elbow jacket, his lumberjack shirt and patched trousers he was once more, if not the poor relation then the impecunious friend of this darling of the fates. Shulepnikov was wearing a magnificent brown leather American combat-type jacket, adorned with numerous zip-fasteners. Jackets of this kind could sometimes be found in secondhand clothes shops, but very rarely, and they cost a mint of money. Glebov could not even dream of buying one, although he constantly pined for one. In those days he was often at Sonya Ganchuk's home, where a fairly select crowd tended to gather and where he didn't yet feel sufficiently self-assured, even though he was an old friend of Sonya's, and he longed passionately for just such a jacket. It had everything: masculinity, elegance, the last word in fashion, practicality. God knows what he would have given for one. As he talked to Lev he could not take his eyes off its soft leather folds. Lev was telling him something about Germany, about a failed marriage, about his father, about the house where he now lived: across Gorky Street from the Central Telegraph Office, over a cocktail bar. Glebov, too, brought him up to date on his life. They talked in tough-sounding voices about tough times. The war had knocked all the boyish illusions out of them, or at least so they thought.

In fact, they were both still boys.

Glebov said, 'That's a really smashing jacket you're wearing. Where can one get them?'

'No problem.'

'No, honestly – where can I get one?'

'I'll ask the old man; he'll say the word to an operator he knows . . .'

Two hours later they were sitting on high stools in the cocktail bar – it was the first time Glebov had been there, and he thought the stools were stupid and uncomfortable, more like perches for birds and as they swung their legs, chain-smoked and gradually got drunk on very strong cocktails, they told each other about their stormy adventures of the past seven years. And there was plenty to tell. Glebov had been evacuated to Glazov, where his mother had collapsed and died in the street from a heart attack. When it happened, Glebov had been in the forest, working in a lumber camp, and he knew nothing about it. Lev had flown to Stamboul on some diplomatic mission, and from there he had been sent to Vienna with a false passport. Glebov came back from the forest after his mother's funeral; he then almost died himself, from inflammation of the lungs, and was nursed back to health by his grandmother. Then his father returned from the front, having been wounded in the head, unable to do any work that demanded the slightest mental effort. He got a job as a stamp-press operator in a small workshop. Walrus had died in the fighting around Leningrad. The Bear and Chemist had vanished without a trace. Virtually everyone from the big house had been scattered to the four winds. Sonya Ganchuk was the only exception. Shulepa's wife had been an Italian woman, Maria, a creature of rare beauty. In Glazov, people had died of starvation; Glebov had had to learn to eat soup made of grass and to drink acorn tea. Maria had been seven years older than Lev Shulepa. At one time he had preferred older women, but then he began to find them boring; they tended to develop complexes. No, Glebov's women had all been younger – all of them, except one. She was absolutely unique . . . well, some other time, maybe; it was a long story. And when did Anton die? Apparently in the autumn of forty-two. It was incredible that he was mobilised at all: he was chronically sick, shortsighted and prone to epileptic fits. And he had very bad hearing. What? Anton had very bad hearing? Of course – you remember how in school he always asked for questions to be repeated and he sat in the front row. But he was amazingly musical – he knew the whole of *Aïda* from memory. Well, so what? Wasn't Beethoven deaf? Yes, it was really sad about Anton. He was a genius. Of course, he was a genius – and in the Leonardo da Vinci mould, a 'renaissance man'. An absolute genius, say what you like. Ought to go and visit his mother. Apparently they had a very hard time in evacuation. But his mother still lives in the same ground-floor flat, on the central courtyard. The one with the cockroaches. Lev had shot a quartermaster of the Allied forces, was court-martialled and threatened with the firing squad, but later it turned out that this quartermaster was a dubious character who had had links with the German

Abwehr, and there was talk of giving Lev a medal, but he didn't get it. Obviously this was a pack of lies, but at the time Glebov believed every word of it and was so thrilled to have met Shulepa again that he was prepared to shell out the last of his cash for another drink, but this was unnecessary – Lev paid. And still Glebov longed for one of those leather jackets.

They then loafed around the Telegraph Office, insulted passers-by, tried to pick up women, and Lev bragged as a policeman watched them complacently without interfering: 'They all know me around here. They're only hoping that I won't touch them . . .'

He frowned and shook a threatening finger at the policeman. Then they went up to his apartment on the third floor, where they had some more drinks. Lev's mother, Alina Fyodorovna, had remained absolutely unchanged since pre-war days. It was astonishing: everything around her had changed, Lev had grown into a hefty young man and was already going bald; Glebov's mother had died, he himself had almost died, at first in Glazov from inflammation of the lungs, then on several occasions when the Germans bombed the airfield; countless other people had died and disappeared – yet Lev's mother was utterly unchanged, with her dark, sunken cheeks, her endless cigarettes, and her strange, frowning, sideways stare.

'Do forgive such a trite question, Vadim, but are you married yet? You're not? Well done – you were always sensible. You're not offended if I call you by your first name, are you?'

The voice was unchanged, too: husky, lazy, with a very slight aristocratic burring of the letter 'R'. Although she was a remarkable and highly intelligent woman (Lev used to say: 'I admire my mother, she is very gifted in her way – but she has a character like Ivan the Terrible'), he felt she could have treated him more like a grown-up. Glebov wanted to behave with dignity. His answers were brief, his smile restrained, and he carefully did not stare at the carpets, the pictures and the knick-knacks that were scattered everywhere, as though he did not notice them at all. Later, having taken a look around, he discovered that the furnishings of the rooms were noticeably different from those in the flat in the big house: the luxury was even more splendid, there were more antiques and a great deal of things connected with the sea. There were models of sailing ships on top of the bookcase, here a framed seascape, there a picture of a sea battle that might well have been by Aivazovsky (it later turned out that it really was by Aivazovsky), and a pattern of gilded anchors on the walls. He said: 'I don't see any of your old furniture, Alina Fyodorovna. Everything appears to be different.'

If he had not been half drunk at that moment he wouldn't have allowed himself to make such an impertinent remark and in such a familiar tone, but something inside egged him to speak out. After all, people during the war had sold their last possessions in order not to starve to death – Nila, Glebov's grandmother, had sold her silver spoons, a silver glass-holder, a rug and several shawls, everything of the slightest value that they had brought with them from Moscow, even the little cross that she wore around her neck, because Glebov was dying and a litre of milk in the market cost approximately the value of a silver spoon – yet here was a newly acquired collection of valuables including an Aivazovsky. To be able to acquire an Aivazovsky was no joke. Glebov purposely went over to the wall and began to inspect the picture intently, leaning close to it like a connoisseur. Lev laughed.

'Look how observant he is. No, Mother, you may say he's drunk, but he has a sharp pair of eyes.'

Alina Fyodorovna said, 'The ancients used to say: No man should step twice into the same stream. That's right, isn't it? I'm not mistaken, am I, young man? You, Vadim, stepped into our stream' – she linked her son and herself with a gesture – 'in roughly what year was it? It must have been when we moved into that awful house, in thirty-something-or-other . . .'

'Well, the exact date doesn't matter. It was about ten years ago,' said Glebov. 'But I remember your flat very well. In the dining room, I remember, there was a huge mahogany sideboard, with an upper part that was supported on thin, spiral columns. And on the doors of the lower part there were some little oval majolica plaques, with pictures of shepherdesses and sheep, cows and things. Am I right?'

'Yes, we did have a sideboard like that,' said Alina Fyodorovna. 'I had forgotten about it, but you remember.'

'Well done!' Lev slapped Glebov on the shoulder. 'Hellishly observant, fabulous memory. You can get a job with talent like that. I'll give you an introduction . . .'

When they were alone in the room, Lev explained that Alina now had another husband. Shulepnikov had died, and this flat with all its costly junk belonged to Fiveisky, Alina Fyodorovna's new husband. He too was a big wheel. He had, in fact, investigated the case of Shulepnikov's death: the latter had died in strange circumstances – he was found dead in his car inside a locked garage. It might have been murder by carbon monoxide, or he might have simply had a heart attack. He had, after all, constantly worked round the clock for years. Fiveisky had investigated the case, and so had come to know Lev's mother. Glebov almost asked why they hadn't brought the furniture from the old place over to Fiveisky's apartment. Things were slightly vague on this point. In Lev's life there were many things that were vague. Better not to ask. Lev said that his new 'dad' was all right – former navy man, fond of drinking and chasing ballerinas. He had once invited Lev to an actors' party, which had been very nice, but everyone there was a bit on the old side. Fiveisky was sixty, but incredibly fit. Glebov asked: 'What about your mother? How does she take his interest in ballerinas?' Lev shrugged his shoulders: 'How is she to know about it? It's a purely male matter.'

Glebov heard this with some amazement, then he brushed it aside: to hell with them, let them live how they like. But something nagged at him, irritated him, as though an old scab had begun to itch intolerably. Later he saw this Fiveisky person three or four times at the apartment in Gorky Street and once at the Dynamo Stadium. Fiveisky was a rabid soccer fan and acted as 'godfather' to some special team, to which (thanks to his connections) he attracted the best players from other clubs. For a while Lev, too, was badly bitten by this nonsense. His new 'dad' was a man of huge stature who talked in a deafening voice and shook hands with a grip like a vice; he also had a head as bald as a peeled peanut, drooping Ukrainian-Cossack moustaches, and with all that he wore gold-rimmed spectacles; in a word – a character.

The big house on the embankment, which played such a significant part in Glebov's earlier life – it had oppressed him, thrilled him, caused him agonies, yet had irresistibly attracted him like a magnet – had now, since the war, relapsed into the shadows. There was no one there now to visit except Sonya

Ganchuk. At first, however, he did not go to see Sonya (for a long time Sonya belonged, as it were, to his childhood, which had gently faded away in his memory along with everything else that had become surplus mental baggage and had been forgotten under the weight of the years) but visited her father, the professor. This was a pure coincidence, which Glebov had discovered casually and with mild interest. It was not until he had been studying at the institute for about eighteen months that he made up his mind to say to the professor: 'You and I, Nikolai Vasilievich, are old acquaintances in a way. I used to come to your home when I was a boy.' Leafing through a book, the professor drawled indifferently: 'You don't say?' And that, on this occasion, was that. The professor had either not understood him or had pretended not to understand.

Glebov was not particularly embarrassed, and decided to remind him more firmly – he was not very interested in Sonya, but Professor Ganchuk himself was an important figure. He, Glebov guessed, could be extremely valuable to him in his early days at the institute – and one day after a lecture he seized a suitable moment and sent his regards to Sonya.

'How do you know Sonya?' Ganchuk said with astonishment.

'But I told you, Nikolai Vasilievich . . .'

'Really? Did you? Oh yes, of course. That's right, I remember, there were always lots of youngsters in our house.'

'And that row of little white busts of the great philosophers – is it still in your study?'

'Well now – you even remember those busts.' The professor smiled with pleasure . . .

Life was getting back to normal. There were still ration cards, but gradually more of life's little pleasures were returning. Yes, the busts were still there. They had survived the war, evacuation, hardships, the destruction of people and ideas – that's because they were, after all, philosophers. For some reason Ganchuk was especially delighted and grew quite enthusiastic when Glebov recalled those little plaster busts – in fact he was much more delighted than when Glebov mentioned his childhood friendship with Sonya. He at once invited Glebov to visit: 'Come up for tea sometime; Sonya will be so pleased . . .'

Later, Sonya too sent her regards, followed by an

invitation. Ganchuk was often ill, and people frequently went to his flat for consultations or to hand in their essays.

Sonya had grown into a tall, pale, rather thin girl, with pale, full lips and big pale-blue eyes that radiated kindness and concern. She was studying at the Institute of Foreign Languages.

'Vadim, what happened to you? What does this mean?' were her first words after six years of separation. 'Why did you disappear so completely?' She said it as though, on parting, they had promised each other to be friends forever. Then and now, however, their relationship was purely and hopelessly one of comradeship, as flat and unemotional as a brick wall. Sonya was just one more element of that bright, variegated, multifaceted, vanished world known as child-hood. And if Professor Ganchuk had not reappeared on the scene, no doubt Sonya would have disappeared forever down the memory hole.

Glebov sat in the professor's study on a little chaise-longue with its hard, curved mahogany back – in those days little settees like this could be had for a song in secondhand shops, though nowadays you can't buy them for love or money – engaged in a pleasurable discussion of the innumerable literary cliques and factions of the 1920s – the fellow travellers, the formalists, the RAPPists, the 'Proletcult' movement – and many other topics in which Glebov was deeply interested. The professor was a mine of information and fascinating detail. He had a particularly clear memory for all the twists and turns of the literary skirmishes and pitched battles of the 'twenties and 'thirties. He spoke crisply and decisively: 'At this point we dealt a heavy blow to the Bespalov group . . . They were backsliders, and had to be hit hard . . . We fought them head-on . . .' Yes, in those days there really were *fights*, not arguments. True understanding was thrashed out in the cut and thrust of polemics. Glebov listened respectfully, imagining the clash of battle, the smashing of idols, the books flung overboard into the raging sea – and this solid, plump, little old man seemed to be some heroic, legendary warrior – which was, in some way, not far from reality. Glebov greatly enjoyed those tea-drinking sessions in the professor's study with their intimate recollec-tions: 'By the way, we disarmed him, and do you know how? As a scholar he was a complete nonentity, but he kept his job thanks to a certain female person . . .' Glebov loved the smell of the carpets and old books, the circle of light thrown on the ceiling by the huge lampshade of the table lamp, he loved the walls lined with books from floor to ceiling and on the very top shelf the little plaster busts lined up in a row like soldiers. Which of them was Plato, which Aristotle? It was impossible to distinguish them from below, because the ceilings in that house were very high, not like the ones they build nowadays, probably at least twelve feet in height. Glebov had the feeling that these indistinguishable little white statuettes – this schoolroom adornment – had been acquired in Germany during the inflation of the mid-1920s, when the eager young Ganchuk, the recent Red Army soldier, committed poet and orator at army political meetings, had plunged into higher learning with the undimmed keenness of a bright boy in high school – these toy sages also took part in the battles, struck blows, lashed out, exposed their opponents and ordered them to lay down their arms.

Gradually and in a new and different way Glebov crept back into the aura of the big house on the embankment. There were no longer any lift men in the entrance hallways, and the tenants were somehow not the same as before; they looked shabbier and simpler and they talked differently. As before, however, the lift shafts were full of unusual smells: shish-kebab, something fishy and tomato-ish, sometimes expensive cigarettes, sometimes dogs. Glebov had grown unaccustomed to dogs over the war years; dogs had somehow been left behind in his childhood, along with ice cream in round wafers, swimming off a sand-spit in the river, and all sorts of other trivia. In the lift on the Ganchuks' entrance, Glebov saw a dog for the first time in years and he examined it carefully. It was a huge Alsatian, yellowish with black streaks, sitting with calm dignity against the back wall of the lift, under the mirror, and it studied Glebov with equal intentness. Alongside the dog, holding it on a lead, stood a despondent-looking old woman in a head scarf. Glebov was amazed by the enormous dog's quietness and well-mannered behaviour, yet at the same time he seemed to detect in its unblinking, nut-brown eyes an awareness of calm superiority: the dog, after all, lived in this house and Glebov was only a visitor. He felt an involuntary urge, a naive movement

49

prompted by childhood memories, to stroke the dog. He stretched out his hand, but the dog growled, shook its muzzle and bared its teeth. 'Hands off! Stand to attention!' – was written on the arrogant black muzzle: 'Just because you are allowed into this house and are going up in this lift does not mean that you belong here.' Glebov got out at the eighth floor landing in a bad mood.

'It smells of dog in your lift,' he said to Sonya.

There were moments when he wanted to needle her.

His life in those days was hard, hungry and fun, as it was for many others; when one thinks back, it was a time of true poverty. There was never an extra pair of shoes, never a spare shirt or tie. And one was perpetually hungry. Everywhere Glebov went – to the institute, visiting friends – he wore his old army tunic, not only because he had nothing else suitable (he had grown out of all his pre-war clothes and could buy nothing new), but also to remind people that he had been *in the war*. He had been conscripted in the last year of the war and had served in the Air Force as ground crew. After the death of his mother, life at home became even drearier than before. His father took to drink. Old Nila, his grandmother, slaved away to the limit of her strength to keep the household going. Looking back, he could not understand how on earth she had managed it. Once a week Nila would take her string bag and take the tram to the Danilovsky market for greens, dried mushrooms, sorrel and rose-hips. God, the gallons of rose-hip tea they drank! Nowadays he couldn't stand the stuff at any price, but in those days Nila even offered him cold rose-hip tea as a cure for hangovers: 'Drink some rose-hip, dear, it'll do you good . . .' Do him good! And yet in a way it must have done him some good, as did everything about that life on their dark, perpetually twilit little street, in their one long, low-ceilinged room that was more like an underground vault – because they kept going, they survived. Grandmother grew more and more bent, walked ever more slowly and began to go faster downhill. Father started working overtime, for which he earned at the rate of time-and-a-half. It was then that his affliction started to get worse. Yet nobody seemed to notice it – he was just always in a hurry to get out and join some friends, to spend his last money on Saturday evenings in some cheap restaurant or in the bar on the Serpukhovka.

Whenever Glebov visited the Ganchuks, he acted the

serious, dedicated academic. At first it was done gropingly, as though feeling his way. Sonya actually hindered him, as she was always wanting to drag him away from her father to talk to her friends, and other irrelevancies.

He also began to get slightly alarmed. Surely, he thought, poor Sonya couldn't be making a play for him? He had no thoughts of anything more intimate than to be praised by the professor, and then entirely within the framework of the syllabus for his degree. Yet at an early stage he had formed an image of himself as a figure dangerously attractive to the female heart. It had begun with a forty-year-old woman during the evacuation. At first he had thought that for her it was just as transient an affair as it was for him, but then passions rose and there were stupid threats. Lord, what a fright that gave him! It taught him to be on his guard: games of that sort could end in tears. He sensed in himself – not without a certain self-satisfaction – a sort of radioactive charge, to which women were prone to fall victim, although not just any women but those of a certain kind. He had a particularly devastating effect on intellectual women who were older than he was, as well as on younger, serious-minded ones who tended to be not very pretty and wore spectacles; when he began teaching, it was usually his best female students who fell under his spell.

It was for this reason that he became slightly nervous whenever he noticed a certain gleam in Sonya's kindly, pale-blue eyes and a slight smile on her full, pale lips. Sonya loved to invite guests home. Among them were her girl friends from the Institute of Foreign Languages, brilliant, brightly dressed girls who twittered and giggled, showing off their fashions; some of them aroused instant and painful longings in Glebov, but he restrained himself, knowing that his brand of radioactivity never worked on such women.

When Glebov became secretary of Ganchuk's seminar, he started visiting them almost every week. The professor was classically absent-minded and, to be honest, hopelessly muddled. They would occasionally have the most absurd and irritating conversation, when the professor would open the door wearing his pyjamas and with eyes round with astonishment would say: 'But my dear fellow, I asked you to come on Monday!'

'No, Nikolai Vasilievich, you said Saturday.'

'How could I have said Saturday, when I . . .'

'But I remember it quite distinctly.'

All this took place in the doorway. The stupidity of it made Glebov feel increasingly nervous, until Sonya suddenly swooped into view: 'Father, you ought to be ashamed of yourself, making people stand in the doorway like this. Have you gone mad?' In actual fact, Ganchuk was always glad to see Glebov and would immediately find him something useful to do. He became particularly well disposed towards Glebov after the latter brought him a complete bibliography on a topic that was important for Ganchuk's own work, and that he had compiled remarkably quickly. Ganchuk was touched by this devotion. Glebov did not tell him that he had worked on it for several nights in a row. He was by no means obliged to exert himself so hard – indeed, he wasn't obliged to compile the bibliography at all – but as it turned out, this feat proved to be amazingly useful.

One evening, Sonya gave a party for a collection of girls and young men of various sorts who turned up, God knows where from, as was usual in those hungry days, to take advantage of the professor's food and drink. Some of the girls brought their friends, who in turn brought theirs. Fortunately, the professor's drawing room was big enough to accommodate fifty people; nowadays rooms of that size are unheard of, except perhaps in flats in privately financed housing schemes. Among the guests were some musicians, a chess champion, and a poet who deafened people at student parties with his crashingly metallic verses – in those days, for some reason, they were regarded as highly musical – and there was the usual gaggle of colourless, loud, shy or insolent students. The poet hit the party like a bolt from the blue: no one knew him, apart from one man who had a fleeting acquaintance with one of the girls and who had never been to Sonya's home before. Hardly had the poet entered the room than he asked in a loud voice, copying the example of certain more famous poets: 'Where's the bog?' This produced a rustle of excited half-whispers: 'He's a poet . . . doing it for effect . . . thoroughly unconventional . . .' No one remembered any of the poems that he recited all evening in a loud, tinny voice, but the remark about the bog . . . Nowadays, thirty years later, the poet is still grinding out his brassy verse, but no one any longer thinks it musical – just tinny. One of the students, after vamping a few chords, started singing in a piercing, hysterical shriek:

> *The Moor of Venice, one Othello,*
> *Called upon his love one day . . .*

Everyone roared in cheerful chorus:

> *Shakespeare, an observant fellow,*
> *Saw him there and wrote a play . . .*

People in those days loved this kind of nonsense. They roared until they were hoarse, until tears came into their eyes:

> *Desdemona was his lady's name,*
> *Most beautiful of all by far . . .*
> *Admiring of Othello's fame,*
> *Bedazzled by his general's stars . . .*

What on earth was there in this junk that was so exciting, that set your heart beating faster, gave you such pleasure that you wanted to share it with others?

There were, however, other parties at the Ganchuks' when different songs were sung around the pale, gently smiling, silent figure of Sonya: her father would come and join the young people in tossing back his glass of lemon-flavoured vodka, Sonya's mother, Yulia Mikhailovna, would sit down with them, and to the beat of the old man conducting with a fork they would all sing 'Through the valleys, over mountains, the division marched ahead . . .' or 'Far away, across the river . . .'

Sonya could sit in silence for hours, listening to other people with her mouth half open, a habit caused by her adenoids, which had not been removed. Once it occurred to Glebov that she would make someone an excellent wife, the best wife in the world. She had so many superlative qualities, up to and including the ability to listen to others in silence with her mouth half open. He thought about this in an absent-minded and disinterested spirit, without making the slightest connection with himself; he might say to himself, for instance: 'Now Sonya would be an excellent wife for Lev.' There actually was a time when he played with this idea, imagining that Sonya might exert a good influence on that blockhead Lev, and that the latter might have a calming effect on the bright-blue gleam of Sonya's eyes, which so alarmed Glebov. Lev couldn't possibly, after all, find any objection if he were to put the idea to him. Glebov himself never felt the slightest desire for a grope with Sonya in a dark corner, as happened with other girls, even with some of those who came to Sonya's parties – for instance with one of her girl friends from the IFL, a dark-eyed, plump little creature – what was her name? He'd forgotten her name, but he had a vivid memory of the touch of her well-covered shoulders, a second's furtive caress in the darkness of a cloakroom, hung all around with soft fur coats . . .

The fact was that with some women he got cold feet and retreated primly into stony reserve, while with others he would suddenly and incomprehensibly behave aggressively and boldly, quite unlike his usual self. He had picked out that plump girl at once; she too lived in a little alleyway like Deryugin Street. Sonya, however, was completely out of it as far as he was concerned; with her he didn't have to make any effort to let himself go, because she had never excited him at all. Later, there came a time when he wanted this to happen; later still, Sonya began to arouse him, but probably two years went by before he reached that stage.

At the party with the poet – it was then that he started to feel the first little glimmerings of interest in Sonya – there was too much alcohol around and people got drunk, to the point where the host and hostess began to worry. Some of the men went out to the hallway to smoke. There was one kid there (Glebov had forgotten his name, of course; he never appeared on the scene again anyway), a clumsy, curly-haired lout in spectacles and a tie. He seemed extremely fit; in fact, there was something of the weight-lifter about him, and in a surprisingly thin, high-pitched voice he suddenly said in the group of men smoking in the hallway: 'I don't quite get it, fellows. Who's getting his leg over our hostess, this bird Sonya?' The kid just wanted to know whether the post was vacant, but his tone was rude and out of place and grated on everyone else's ears. People shrugged their shoulders. Then one of the students nodded towards Glebov. 'Could be comrade Vadim here . . .'

'Me?' said Glebov in amazement. 'That's news to me.'

It was a nasty moment: other people had noticed something of which he himself wasn't aware, something which in any case had never crossed his mind. Or had it? He found himself telling them that he and Sonya had been classmates at school. The boy who had started the conversation said: 'Who wants to, anyway. She might as well be a nun in a convent.' He nodded towards the open door into the flat. 'Too much like hard work . . . Still, there's something about her . . . you know, like one of Turgenev's women.'

'Shut up, slob,' said someone.

The weight-lifter took offence, threw away his cigarette end and went back into the flat. Nobody liked him.

'Who brought that thug here?'

'God knows. I think he's from the Literary Institute.'

'Shall we give him the treatment?'

They agreed. One of them went inside to get him to come out in the hallway again. He was gone for some while, and when he did return he said the body builder had guessed they wanted to beat him up and refused to come. All right, they decided; they'd give him the treatment later. He wouldn't get away from them. The chess champion was particularly fierce. They had all had a lot to drink. Something unusual, however, happened to Glebov: he suddenly and oddly became completely sober. He was sobered up by the thought that that boy had expressed in such a crude way. 'He's not a fool,' thought Glebov. '*We* are the fools.' This made him feel an even stronger urge to rough him up – well, maybe not rough him up but just throw him out. 'He slithers in here where he doesn't belong . . . Sneaky bastard!'

Glebov strode angrily into the drawing room. They never did rough up the kid in glasses, for the simple reason that within half an hour he was dead drunk. At twelve-thirty the guests said goodbye, hoping to catch the last metro. They all left except the bespectacled weight-lifter, who could not even be pulled off the divan, much less put on his feet; he lay sprawled in a revolting attitude, showing all the patches on his threadbare student's trousers, with his sweater rucked up and a gap between belt and sweater revealing his navel amid an expanse of bare stomach. He had thrown his arms behind his head, which was hanging over the bolster at the end of the divan, and he was snoring horribly. It turned out that the man who had brought him had long since left with his girl friend, a student friend of Sonya's. No one even knew what his name was. The Ganchuks were in a quandary. Vasyona, the maid, advised sending for the police. With her solid German common sense that had survived thirty years of living in Russia, Yulia Mikhailovna suggested putting a glass of water and an aspirin tablet alongside the sleeping youth. Vasyona snorted with indignation: 'Aspirin tablet indeed . . . As soon as he wakes up he'll start looking for the way out and he'll smash the glass in the bookcases in the middle of the night . . .' Old Ganchuk himself was all for using the old army method – dragging him out by the ears. Sonya, however, came to the defence of the drunken lout and forbade them to touch him.

'Don't you feel sorry for him? Look at his nice little face and that sweet bulldog's jaw.'

Glebov suggested firmly that he should stay for the night, just in case; he would sleep here in the living room on the camp-bed, and that character could stay on the divan – only they ought to take his shoes off.

So Glebov spent the night in Sonya's flat; for a long time he could not sleep, because he had started to think about Sonya in a quite new and different way. He just lay there unable to sleep, and thinking. Now and again he dozed off, dreamed short, muddled dreams, woke up again and once more started thinking. Little happened; Sonya slept in her own room behind a firmly shut door and the drunkard did not stir; what did happen happened to Glebov that night, for he got up a different person the next morning. He realised that he could fall in love with Sonya. The feeling as such had not yet manifested itself, but it was somewhere on the way, getting nearer, like a mass of warm air billowing in from the south. People with vascular trouble can feel the onset of a change in the weather before it comes. At dawn, around six o'clock in the morning, the lout turned over, fell on the floor and began, as Vasyona had predicted, to blunder around the room, muttering and hiccuping. Glebov dragged him out into the hallway, jammed his cap on his head and tried to shove him out of the front door. The unwanted guest refused to go; and they swore at each other in whispers:

'Where are you pushing me, you monster? I don't have anywhere to go, don't you see?'

'Go back where you came from.'

'Where I came from? Can't you understand what Dostoyevsky wrote . . .? When a person has nowhere to go . . .'

In those days there were quite a few such semi-destitute students who practically lived on the streets. They were constantly shunted along as they tried to cadge a night's sleep from friends, sneaked from one student hostel to another, slept in railway stations. Now this student clung longingly to this haven from which he was being thrown out. Glebov spend a good half-hour persuading him to go, and finally pushed him out, after which he returned to the drawing room and lay down on the camp bed. An hour later Sonya walked past in her dressing down. He saw her pale thin legs and slender ankles. Later she looked in again and asked: 'What happened to him?'

'I gave him the heave-ho.' Glebov made a movement with his knee depicting a push in the posterior. He felt himself a hero, a protector of the weak, but to his surprise Sonya was angry.

'Who asked you to do that? He didn't want to go, did he?'

'No, he didn't. I spent an hour in the hall trying to get rid of him.'

'And you threw him out? How horrible of you, Vadim. You ought to be ashamed of yourself. Kicking out a hungry man. Maybe he didn't have anywhere to go . . .'

'He didn't have. Because he's a bum.'

'I don't know what that is.'

'But I know. I live among them. Deryugin Street is full of bums.'

Sonya only shook her head, giving him a new, mistrustful look, and went back to her room, obviously displeased. Glebov did not know what to do. Should he go? Sonya's annoyance surprised him. Later, when he came to know her better, he realised that the chief trait in her character was an almost morbid, unselective proneness to pity others – anybody, no matter who or what they were. At times he found this characteristic tedious, even painful, but later he got used to it and stopped paying it any attention. Her first reaction to any real-life confrontation with people was to pity them. He would tease her about it: 'Oh, I feel so sorry for that poor mugger who beat up three people at a tram stop . . . Just imagine the agony in his soul . . .' Sonya herself was aware of the absurdity of this side of her nature and it pained her.

When they sat down to breakfast, just the two of them, at a little round table by a window, she was embarrassed and tried to make excuses for her earlier bad-tempered outburst: 'If only you had given him a cup of tea.'

'Don't worry,' said Glebov. 'He'll survive anyway. His kind always does.'

He looked down at the gigantic curve of the bridge, with cars and trams rolling across it, at the far bank of the river with the Kremlin wall, palaces, fir trees, gilded domes – it was all astonishingly picturesque and somehow looked unusually fresh and clear from this height – and it occurred to him that clearly a new phase in his life was beginning.

To have a bird's-eye view of all those palaces every morning at breakfast! And to pity all those people, all of them without exception, running like little ants across the concrete arc down below. It was all a continuation of his half-waking, half-dozing semi-delirium of last night's thoughts. He said, 'Know what? You'd do better to feel sorry for *me*.'

'I do, too.' She stroked his cheek. 'You're so restless, a kind of lost soul.'

He began to visit the Ganchuks almost every day, sometimes to see the professor, sometimes Sonya. Before, the professor had called him 'my dear fellow' and 'Vadim Alexandrovich', but now he began calling him by the affectionate form of his first name, Dima. He invited him to join him on his evening walks. Whenever he donned his black Persian-lamb hat, slipped on his white Caucasian cloak patched with chocolate-brown leather or put on his long-skirted overcoat lined with fox fur, he looked like a nineteenth-century Russian merchant in one of Ostrovsky's plays. But that merchant, strolling along the deserted evening embankment with measured, unhurried steps, would describe the Polish campaign, the difference between the Cossack trooper's and the officer's sabre-stroke, the relentless struggle against petty-bourgeois counterrevolution and anarchistic elements, and would discuss Lunacharsky's theoretical errors, the delusions of Pokrovsky, the vacillations of Gorky, the mistakes of Alexei Tolstoy: Ganchuk had known them all, had drunk tea with them, stayed at their *dachas*. And although he spoke about all of them with respect, even when discussing such famous men as Gorky, his tone of voice also carried a hint of hidden superiority, as though he possessed some additional knowledge: 'If only Gorky had fully understood . . .' he would say, or, 'As I once explained to Alexei Tolstoy . . .'

Glebov listened to Ganchuk with great attention. It was all interesting and important. Sometimes Nikolai Vasilievich staggered Glebov with an astonishing remark. For instance, when describing his *dacha* out at Bruskovo and the troubles in getting to it (the village Soviet had taken a disgracefully long time over asphalting the road), he ended quite unexpectedly by saying: 'In five years' time every Soviet citizen will have a *dacha*.' Glebov was amazed at this statement but made no objections.

There were evenings of fierce twenty-five-degree frost, when sensible people preferred to stay at home, but sharp at nine Nikolai Vasilievich would wrap himself in a scarf, ram his hat down to his eyebrows, envelop himself in his merchant's fur coat and demand: 'Are you coming with me?' How Glebov wanted not to go out into the cold! To slip through sheltered backyards to his house was one thing, but to stroll along the windy, icebound embankment . . . Glebov would answer with doomed acquiescence: 'Of course, of course. I'm ready.' He shivered and hunched himself up in his thin student's overcoat (cut down from an old one of his father's), restrained himself from breaking into a run and made himself keep a steady pace alongside the old man, who huffed and puffed pleasurably in his warm fur coat. 'What a selfish, inconsiderate old brute,' Glebov sometimes thought with annoyance. 'It never occurs to him . . .' And another thought crossed his mind: Perhaps the professor was taking him out of the house on purpose, so that he wouldn't be left alone with Sonya?

Another guess was suggested to him by Vasyona. The crafty old peasant woman, who noticed everything, one day asked him sympathetically, 'Why does he always drag you out with him? I think it's because he's keeping a kind of eye on you . . .'

'Is he guarding me, or am I guarding him?' asked Glebov. Vasyona whispered, 'I don't know, but there are people around here who don't like people like that who wear fur coats.'

Occasionally Sonya, too, would come walking with them,

59

and they would be joined by Kuno Ivanovich, or Kunik as he was known; a close friend of the Ganchuks, he was Nikolai Vasilievich's assistant in his work at the Academy. This Kunik was treated by the Ganchuks almost like a relative. Glebov noticed that Nikolai Vasilievich was not very fond of taking Sonya with him, and whenever Kuno Ivanovich insisted on coming he paid no attention to him. The reason turned out to be quite simple: when only Glebov was there, Nikolai Vasilievich would blossom into eloquence, told stories and reminisced without drawing breath, but when Sonya was with them, he was bored and silent. She was always liable to say crossly, 'Be quiet, Papa. You mustn't talk when it's so cold'. Or, 'Papa, you're repeating yourself'.

Yulia Mikhailovna, however, did not like the streets, the cars, the wind and frosts. She had stenosis of the coronary arteries. She was often too unwell to go to work: Yulia Mikhailovna taught German at the same institute in which Glebov studied and where Professor Ganchuk was chairman of a department. Although she had lived in Russia for several decades, Yulia Mikhailovna remained in some ways a tough, unbending German woman and spoke Russian with a noticeable accent. Her father had died during the Hamburg uprising. Yulia Mikhailovna still kept contact with several old anti-Fascists – Germans and Austrians – who had survived many hazards and hardships and who now and again appeared at the Ganchuks'. Kuno Ivanovich came from this milieu. His mother, who had died before the war, had been an old friend of Yulia Mikhailovna from their days together at the University of Vienna, and the Ganchuks had for years acted as Kunik's guardian, having known him since he was a boy. Kunik. It was like the name of a dog – a small, spoiled little lap-dog with intelligent little eyes.

'Kunik has to be fed,' Sonya used to say.

'Ask Kunik . . . Ring up Kunik . . . We must send Kunik to get tickets, but very tactfully . . .'

Thin and stooping, he held his head a little low and to one side as though he were permanently listening to something, although he never listened to anything and often failed to hear when people spoke to him. Now and again he would twitch his bent head – he probably suffered from a tic – throwing back his long, pale-reddish hair. At first Glebov thought he had tuberculosis.

Glebov disliked Kunik. He was so very taciturn, unfriendly, secretive and wily. Kunik lived alone. The Ganchuks were perpetually worried about him – was he ill? did he need anything? For some reason they had the idea that he always needed help and that he was unhappy. Indeed, the words 'I am unhappy' were written on his mournful, desiccated little face with its thin-lipped mouth. But why was he unhappy?

One day at dinner Glebov cautiously started a conversation about an article that Kunik had published in a journal. He had heard for a long time that the article was in preparation, that the editors were demanding amendments to it, that Kunik was being obstinate and showing an unheard-of adherence to principle, that in his fight with the editor he had found allies in high places and had succeeded in getting the article into print despite all obstacles. In the scholarly world this was being talked of as a major event. Yulia Mikhailovna, in particular, had been closely involved in the whole business. When he had read it, however, Glebov realised that this article was thoroughly mediocre in quality and in no way outstanding, except that it was obvious, from a number of subtle, intangible clues, that Russian was not the author's native tongue. The writing betrayed a general sense of woodenness and lack of vitality. This was, in fact, the topic that he raised at dinner: that unfortunately works on literary history were often written in a language that was far from literary. Nikolai Vasilievich agreed with him, making many slanderous accusations on that score, and only then, after much discussion, did Glebov very gently introduce two or three examples from Kunik's article. The quotations were indeed striking in their lack of understanding of the spirit and style of the Russian language.

Nikolai Vasilievich laughed, Sonya smiled, but Yulia Mikhailovna remarked coldly that if people were going to make such malicious criticism, 'they should make it to the author's face'. Glebov insisted that there was nothing malicious in his comments, but Yulia Mikhailovna objected: 'That is not true, Vadim. Don't be disingenuous. You haven't yet said what you think of Kuno Ivanovich's article as a whole.'

Shrugging his shoulders, Glebov muttered, 'What do I think of it? To be honest . . . I'm not exactly thrilled by it, but on the other hand I'm not . . .'

'Ah! In other words, I was right.' Proudly, Yulia Mikhailovna raised a threatening forefinger. 'And may I ask you . . .?'

But Sonya interrupted her mother: why didn't Glebov have the right to his own opinion, which might be different from the opinion of the Ganchuk family? Why must she immediately attack him? Nikolai Vasilievich remarked that the Ganchuk family by no means shared a single opinion. Yulia Mikhailovna retorted that charging into the attack was the privilege of Nikolai Vasilievich, as a one-time Red cavalry-man, and she was not given to wielding a sword.

'But you do wield a sword,' said Sonya, 'and sometimes very fiercely.'

Glebov wished that he had not started the conversation. The delicate and apparently very weak and sickly Yulia Mikhailovna with her thin little hands and parchment-white face was, it must be said, unusually obstinate. She could argue and insist on her point of view *bis zum Schluss* – until, in fact, she had a heart attack. She said that criticism should above all be objective and should assess the work as a whole, and only then proceed to nit-picking. Kunik had written a splendid article. Minor comments should be confined to small print. He had written about an important topic – the danger of spontaneous petty-bourgeois counterrevolution. It was now in particular, when people wanted to relax and rest after the exhausting victory over Nazism, that petty-bourgeois emotions, hitherto repressed, could flare up again. It was a danger that must not be underestimated.

Glebov had read nothing of the sort in Kunik's article. Timidly, he allowed himself to object: 'Excuse me, Yulia Mikhailovna, but if I made a few comments about the language, that doesn't mean I underestimate the petty-bourgeois danger.'

'Precisely!' said Nikolai Vasilievich, and banged his fist on the table. He tended to reduce most things to a joke. 'The one doesn't follow from the other, for heaven's sake.'

'No, you underestimate the bourgeois danger,' said Yulia Mikhailovna, who was in no mood for flippancy.

'And where do you see it, Yulia Mikhailovna?'

'I'll tell you. Do you want me to be frank? For a long time I've noticed it in you, Vadim . . .' And here she launched on a catalogue of such staggering, unbelievable nonsense that

Glebov was struck dumb with amazement. It appeared that he had always examined everything in their flat with particular interest, that in the kitchen he was unduly fascinated by the refrigerator and the door of the service lift. Once he had questioned her in great detail about the family's *dacha* in Bruskova – how many rooms did it have, was there a piped water supply, how big was the surrounding property in square metres – just as if he had been thinking of buying it.

'Mama! What are you talking about?' exclaimed Sonya in alarm.

'I'm talking about what I notice in the young people of today,' said the obstinate woman, whose heart condition was already making her short of breath from the energetic statement of her principles. 'And it doesn't only apply to Vadim. I happen to like Vadim, and don't want to offend him in any way. Don't worry, Vadim, you and I will still be on the best of terms. But I notice in so many people with such a passion for things, for comforts and possessions, for what the Germans call *das Gut* and the Russians call "goods" . . . Why? What does this apartment have to offer you?' She raised her shoulders and looked around the room with an expression of disdain, almost of abhorrence on her face. 'Do you think you can't work just as well in your little room in that little wooden house of yours? Can't you be happy there?'

'But I haven't noticed you abandoning this place so that you can go and live in a little wooden house,' said Sonya.

'Why should I? It's all the same to me where I live, in a great palace or in a log cabin, if I can live according to my own, inner standards.'

Yulia Mikhailovna was right in that her attitude towards Glebov remained unchanged after these strange accusations. Glebov was determined not to be offended. He had guessed what was behind it all: Sonya's mother harboured a particular sympathy for Kunik, apparently seeing him as an ideal son-in-law, but Sonya had other views on this matter. Without knowing it, Glebov had hit a sore point.

Not without a certain concealed self-satisfaction, he felt that Yulia Mikhailovna's irritation, her digs and verbal attacks were only a sign that the advantage was *on his side*. Her remarks about his alleged petty-bourgeois sins seemed even more enigmatic. He did not for one second feel himself to be guilty of them. Could she really have been serious in what she said? Was it perhaps a carefully staged joke? It could have been significant that Ganchuk himself had made just one remark and then just grinned. And what about the lift, panelled in fake mahogany, with its full-length mirror? Yulia Mikhailovna, after all, never walked upstairs to the ninth floor but rode up and down in that lift, admired herself in the mirror and breathed the aroma of expensive cigarettes, expensive dogs and expensive everything else. Downstairs in the lobby, it was true, you were no longer scrutinised by sharp-eyed lift men in uniforms and caps, but there was an old woman in felt boots sitting there in a broken armchair, and in a lazy, husky voice she asked everyone who entered, 'Which flat are you going to?'

If the Ganchuks' flat in Moscow could make some pretensions to luxury, their *dacha* was a slovenly, almost derelict house, with a rotting roof, an unfinished second storey in which the windows were boarded up with plywood, but even so this house with its grounds of about an acre, its fence, its fir trees, the wild vine around the porch and its little kitchen garden was that same detested private property, that very '*das Gut*' in which petty-bourgeois values flourished like the onions that grew in the vegetable beds.

In spring, when the *dacha* season started again, the Ganchuk family would go out to Bruskovo for a so-called 'working Sunday', at the *dacha*: they worked in the yard, in the house, in the kitchen garden – if you could call it work. Because of her general ill health, Yulia Mikhailovna only fluttered helplessly around and annoyed the others with her muddled instructions; Sonya was lazy and rather clumsy, while Nikolai Vasilievich went straight into the study and disappeared among his old books and papers. All the real work was done by the ancient Vasyona, helped occasionally by Anikeyev the chauffeur, who spent most of the day tinkering with the Ganchuks' car, a Pobieda. This Anikeyev, an elderly, morose man, had been some sort of minor official before the war but had got into trouble. He did everything very slowly, never went anywhere in a hurry, skilfully avoided hard work and chose the easier jobs: he would spend half a day mending a lampshade or nailing a new plank into the fence. Once when Glebov was pushing a wheelbarrow full of rubbish to the far end of the garden – he had eagerly offered his help to Nikolai Vasilievich, being consumed with curiosity to see what the *dacha* was like – Anikeyev whispered to him; 'Let the old woman move the rubbish herself. Didn't you do a deal with her?' He took Glebov for a paid labourer . . .

That summer they were parted. Glebov went to the Kuban to do farm work in remote Cossack villages, and he found himself – unexpectedly – missing Sonya. It was then that he realised the thing was serious.

Around New Year, the winter being mild, a horde of their student friends descended on Bruskovo; they heated the *dacha* and decorated a fir tree in the garden with little coloured electric lights. It was splendid.

It was then that Lev Shulepnikov joined their crowd for the first time; he had been at the institute for a year, then had gone his own way, no one knew where. 'I'm like Kipling's cat,' he said, 'I walk by myself.' He arrived at Bruskovo with a very pretty girl named Stella, a dancer in the then new and ultra-fashionable Beryozka folk-dance troupe.

For some reason, a very long and noisy argument took place. People shouted and yelled, until eventually a fight broke out. The unwitting source of it all was Astrug, a lecturer in linguistics, whom they used to bully and rag mercilessly in lectures. The argument started as a joke: what was the colour of Astrug's underpants? The underlying cause was, of course, something different – quite, quite different! – and it even had nothing really to do with the wretched Astrug, who belonged, incidentally, to Professor Ganchuk's entourage, although on this occasion that had nothing to do with the argument either. It clearly resulted from the build-up of a kind of volcanic pressure of angry frustration, which had been gathering force below the surface, hidden from the casual glance, and now had suddenly burst out. Lev Shulepnikov was, as always, the irritant that sparked the explosion, although he was too frivolous to be aware of what he was doing. There was, of course, a great deal of vodka and nothing to eat – the usual student binge, aggravated by ravenous hunger, tiredness, pre-term nerves and that more sinister volcanic force that was seething deep down inside them.

It all began with a certain Cheremisin, an unpleasant youth who wasn't one of Glebov's friends but had simply shown up along with the others, the gang being a very mixed bunch (whoever put a bottle or two into the kitty was welcome), all

65

in all about twenty people. They had thought beforehand that they could easily fit twenty into the big *dacha* comfortably, but in the event it seemed overcrowded and ended in a fight. When someone started talking about Astrug, Cheremisin told a story about him. It seems that during a test Astrug had asked him, 'What is a morpheme?' Cheremisin didn't know. Astrug said, 'How can you know a language if you don't know what a morpheme is?' At which Cheremisin asked, 'What does *salazgan* mean?' Astrug, of course, shrugged his shoulders. Cheremisin then asked, 'And what is *shurdy-burda?*' The lecturer didn't know that either. 'How can you know the language, Professor, if you don't know such simple words? Where I come from, every old man and every little kid knows them. *Salazgan* means something like riff-raff. And *shurdyburda* means what happens in your lectures – chaos and confusion.' Astrug just laughed, waved his hand and gave Cheremisin a 'C'.

'But on the whole he deserved to be chucked out,' Cheremisin added in conclusion. 'He admires foreign bourgeois scholars too much. He doesn't show it, but he does. That's for sure. He may know the literary language, but he doesn't know a damn thing about the language that real people speak.'

A girl said, 'I don't know, and I don't care, what he knows or doesn't know, but I'm very glad he's going. He makes me sick: sits down on a chair, crosses his legs, swings his foot, and somehow his trousers always manage to get hitched up so far that you can see his long blue underpants tucked into his socks. Ugh, disgusting.' The girl pulled a face of revulsion. 'I couldn't bear to look, so I shut my eyes . . . and nothing that he says goes into your head.'

Cheremisin roared with laughter. 'That's it. Right on the button. But they weren't blue, they were white. I don't remember them being blue.'

'Well, now that he's been sacked he can sit at home and swing his leg,' said the girl.

They began to get heated and quarrelsome, not just because they had drunk too much but also because it wasn't a gathering of friends, rather just a random collection. The girl's from Sonya's institute and their boyfriends made up one element, Glebov's friends comprised another, on top of which there were the gate-crashers and casual hangers-on, such as Cheremisin. The whole bunch hummed, bubbled and boiled, as people met new faces, became instant friends and equally instantly found reasons why they disliked each other. The arguments were shrill and furious. Some of Sonya's girl friends started to tease the girl who had talked about Astrug's underpants. Lev Shulepnikov rudely interrupted Cheremisin: 'You used to lick Astrug's arse and now you sneer at him. That's pretty cheap.' Lev wasn't really as high-minded as he sounded and he didn't give a damn about Astrug (Glebov knew Shulepa inside out), but evidently Cheremisin had annoyed him in some way, either by his impudence or by something else – probably because he had tried to make a pass at the pretty Beryozka girl. Why did he do it? As the subsequent argument revealed, it was simply to annoy Lev. Cheremisin hated Lev. And he wasn't the only one. 'None of us,' shouted Cheremisin, his prominent, high cheekbones turning white with fury, 'give a damn for you with your cars, and your daddies and mummies. To us you're just a nothing – zero! Pfoo!' And to ram it home, he spat at Lev. He might not have actually spat, but at any rate he pretended to spit. The beautiful Stella shrieked. Lev crawled over the table, ready for a fight. People held him back, but it was obvious that there was going to be a big row. Cheremisin had come with two friends from his hostel. Glebov knew them well; one was a decent, harmless kid who belonged to Glebov's crowd – but everyone was so terribly drunk. Up until about two o'clock in the morning, while they were sitting at table, things were still more or less under control, but later, as chairs were pushed back and overturned, people began scrambling out from behind the table; they spread all through the rooms and up to the first floor, tumbled out of doors into the snow – that was where the real trouble began, out in the snow . . . Then they surged back indoors, around the rooms, all over the floor, smashing chairs to a background chorus of screaming women and the tinkle of breaking glass. Glebov, feeling he was in a way the host, tried to separate them, but he didn't do it firmly enough and suffered for his pains: somebody jabbed an elbow into his face, giving him a massive black eye. The wretched Lev's nose was broken, and he went around with a crooked nose for at least six months. People said that the beautiful Stella behaved heroically in defending her boyfriend – she took off a shoe and lashed out at the attackers with the heel, aiming to smash the spectacles of anyone who came within range. The damage and the wounds did not come to light right away – because by dawn anyone who was still on his feet was running hurriedly and shamefacedly to catch the train back into town and Glebov found practically nobody at the *dacha* at breakfast – but became apparent three days later, when they all gathered at the institute for sessions with their supervisors before the next exam.

Back in Bruskovo, however, when the others had all gone and Glebov and Sonya were left alone, something very important happened. The temperature was above zero, with only a gentle snowfall fluttering down. They went out with shovels and cleared the drive. There was never more than twilight all day, and they turned the lights on early. For several hours they worked hard to get the house back into shape, until they were dead tired – Sonya was in a hurry to tidy it up, because she was afraid her parents might arrive – then they sat down in the kitchen and drank tea out of earthenware mugs. Her parents didn't come. The mugs were heavy, chocolate-brown in colour, and the tea was unusually delicious. They remembered those earthenware mugs forever. There was also a moment when Sonya had gone over to the neighbouring *dacha* to take back some borrowed crockery, and he was alone in the loft, the warmest room in the whole house; the window on to the garden was open, letting in the aromas of snow and fir trees and the smoke of burning lime wood, and he lay on the divan, an old-fashioned one with bolsters and a tasselled fringe, put his hands behind his head, stared at the ceiling with its striped wallpaper darkened with age, at the strips of insulating felt that poked out between the planking of the walls, which were adorned with photographs and a little engraving of a scene from the Russo-Turkish war, and suddenly – like a rush of blood to the head, making him dizzy – he had the feeling that all this might become his house. Even now, perhaps – no one had guessed it yet, but he knew – these yellowing boards with their knotholes and photographs, the squeaky window-frame, the snow-covered roof *belonged to him!*

He felt an urgent thirst for something to drink, even if only a mouthful of yesterday's flat beer. He went downstairs, looked everywhere but found nothing. Snow was falling soundlessly. When Sonya returned, he felt a sudden surge of strength. Sonya's eyes were sparkling, her cheeks wet with snow. He kissed her cold lips and cold fingers, murmured that he couldn't live without her. He was seized with real desire, which he had never felt before with Sonya, and this thrilled him. Sonya burst into tears and said, 'Why have we been wasting the whole day?' Although it was still early, only about seven o'clock in the evening, they made up a bed on the divan in the loft, put out the light and fell upon each other naked, unwilling to wait another second. After a little while there suddenly came a knock downstairs, first at the front door, then at the side door on the verandah. It was probably some of their friends, coming back to carry on the party. The knocking was very insistent, and they could hear two or three people walking round the house in the snow, talking and conferring. Someone shouted: 'Vadim! Open up, you sneaky bastard!' Then a girl's voice: 'Sonya, it's us!' Someone else shouted cheerfully: 'Hey, what are you two doing in there?' There was a burst of laughter. Glebov could not recognise them from their voices. Sonya wanted to go down and open the door, but Glebov would not let her: 'Lie quiet!' His arms were around the thin, submissive, soft body, thin shoulders and thin back. There was no weight in this body, but now it belonged to him – or so he felt; it belonged to him along with everything else: the old house, the fir trees, the snow. And he kissed it, caressed it, did whatever he wanted with it, but tried to do it without any noise, while down below they knocked, buzzed like a swarm of bees, swore and went away.

It became unbearably hot that night in the *dacha*. Not knowing how to deal with the boiler properly, he had stoked it with too much coal and created such an inferno that they couldn't sleep. They opened all the windows, but it did little to help. There was a thaw outside, the crust of snow creaked as it began to melt and run down the roof, and there was a continual melting, dripping and tinkling outside the window. Glebov and Sonya threw off the blanket, lay naked on the sheet, groaned at the heat and stuffiness and talked in low voices. They were now completely unembarrassed by each other's bodies. Sonya asked, 'When did you fall in love with me?' This put Glebov on the spot: he truly could not answer with any exactitude; it seemed to have happened quite recently, but he decided not to say so.

He replied, 'What difference does it make? The great thing is that it has happened.'

'Of course,' she whispered, contentedly. 'I just asked because I remember very well when it was . . . And you may have forgotten . . .'

'And when,' he asked, 'did it happen to you?'

To his amazement he learned that she had fallen in love with him as long ago as their school days, when he had first come to her home with the red-haired Yarik and Anton Ovchinnikov and told them about the very intelligent cat he had found ill on the street and how since then the cat had always walked with him to school along the embankment. They had all gone to see the cat at Glebov's apartment. Glebov had completely forgotten the whole episode.

'And I remember when I felt another burst of love for you . . . It only lasted a second, but it was intense and painful but somehow sweet, I remember it clearly . . . You came to school wearing a brown jacket with a belt. It wasn't new, but you never wore it as a rule, that was why I noticed it. I observed you very carefully, you see. And so when you were standing by the window I saw on the back of your jacket a large, carefully sewn-on patch, about as big as the page of a school notebook. You can't imagine how much I loved you at that moment.'

He was offended. Why should she love him because of a patch? He didn't admit that this upset him, but just murmured, 'My grandmother was a genius at sewing on patches.'

Sonya keenly interested, at once asked, 'Oh, your grandmother did it? And for some reason I imagined that it was your mother who was such a good needlewoman.'

Later, Glebov frequently noticed that Sonya had an insatiable interest in every kind of trifle about his childhood, about life with his parents, and was constantly questioning him on all kinds of silly details about his past. The surge of love for him evoked by the patch on his jacket had merged with a secret dream of hers: to raise enough money from somewhere to buy him a new jacket and send it to him with a note reading: 'From an unknown friend'. There had been another unusually strong impression connected with him: love and horror that for a second had fused into one. It had

70

happened once when she had seen him out of the window: Chemist was standing on the narrow ledge of the balcony outside the railings, right over the abyss. And Glebov's face was frozen into such a look of horror, as though Chemist had already fallen and was lying down there on the pavement. Oh, that was a terrible moment. Did he still remember it? Of course he remembered it; that kind of childish madness stuck in the memory for a lifetime.

'And there were a few other minor agonies,' said Sonya. 'For instance, when you were so crazy about that little fool Tamara Mishchenko . . .'

At this he burst out laughing. Who was Tamara Mishchenko? Not that enormous fat girl? They both laughed until they ached.

Next day – which was Sunday – Sonya's parents arrived with Vasyona. Glebov was afraid that they were bound to guess what had happened to their daughter and prepared himself for the worst; it did not, in his view, require any great gift of intuition. Sonya, however, behaved so coolly and naturally, met them so joyfully, looked after them so lovingly and attentively that Glebov was secretly amazed and her parents suspected nothing. Anyway, they were a couple of old fogies. That was the explanation: two nice, decent old fogies – what's more, both of the same sort – completely preoccupied with their own affairs. But what about Vasyona and her sharp eyes? She didn't pick up any clues, either. Later, however, she was the first to guess.

Nikolai Vasilievich was out of sorts that day, gloomy and unaware of anything around him. Lunch passed in an uncomfortable silence. Glebov wondered whether the Ganchuks felt unable to talk freely because he was there. He whispered to Sonya: 'Should I go?'

Sonya shook her head. 'No, of course not. He's just worried about something. It's nothing to do with you.'

After lunch he and Sonya went for a walk. That evening, after taking a nap for a couple of hours, the old man was more relaxed, started talking and explained that he was worried about the business of Astrug's being sacked from the institute. He and Yulia Mikhailovna had been unable to come out to the *dacha* yesterday because the Astrugs, Boris Lvovich and his wife, had suddenly asked to come round and see them. They could hardly refuse them. The Astrugs were utterly crushed – no one had invited them for New Year – so how could they not let them come round? Nikolai Vasilievich had been absent from the meeting of the Faculty Board that had decided on Astrug's expulsion and where, effectively, the rest of the plot had taken shape.

'Do you realise, Vadim, what a dirty trick they played? I was away on a trip!' said Ganchuk, growing more and more heated, while Yulia Mikhailovna, by gesticulating, making faces and adding irritating little remarks, tried to make him talk more calmly or, preferably, stop talking altogether. 'You remember I was away for three and a half weeks in Prague, working in the archives, and they took advantage of my absence . . .'

'But Papa, why should they need to have you out of the way?' asked Sonya.

'What d'you mean "why"? Ridiculous question. Because if I had been there I would have spoken out loudly and firmly against the whole thing.'

'Exactly what they wanted you to do,' said Yulia Mikhailovna.

'Please don't interrupt. You don't understand.'

'No, I do understand. You're the one who doesn't understand what's going on, because you're hardly ever there, whereas I go there every day. It would have suited them very well if you had intervened in this business.'

'Then I shall intervene!' barked Ganchuk.

'There's no longer any point. Absolutely *sinnlos*.'

'We shall see!'

He relapsed into gloom, got up from the tea table and went to his study. Sonya and Glebov climbed the creaking stairs to the loft. Locking the door, and without switching on the light, Sonya flung herself at Glebov, began kissing him and whispering:

'Oh, I feel so sorry for Astrug. My poor, poor, poor, poor Astrug . . .' Each 'poor' was accompanied by a kiss.

'So do I,' he whispered, kissing the tender little hollow above her collar-bone. 'I feel very sorry for him too . . .'

'I simply can't tell you . . . how much I pity Astrug.'

'Me too . . .'

She clasped Glebov with all the strength in her weak arms. He stroked her back, her shoulder-blades and her hips, everything that now belonged to him. They could hear people talking downstairs while Vasyona and Yulia Mikhailovna clattered the dishes. Then Yulia Mikhailovna called out: 'Son-ya!'

Sonya pulled away from Glebov and whispered, 'We're fooling around, but I really do pity him. Don't think I'm kidding. If he comes, you'll get to know him better.'

Glebov wondered what she meant by this. Another shout from below, this time angrily: 'Sonya, what's going on?'

She kissed Glebov and ran downstairs, heels clattering on the staircase. Still without switching on the light, Glebov went over to the window and pushed it open with the palm of his hand. Mist and cold forest air blew over him. From right outside the window the smell of pine needles wafted in from a heavy branch under its greyish covering of snow.

Glebov stood by the window, took a deep breath and thought: 'That branch is mine too!'

Next morning at breakfast, when Anikeyev had already arrived with the car to take the three of them back to Moscow – Ganchuk and Vasyona were to stay for a few more days – the talk turned again to Astrug. Yulia Mikhailovna said, 'All right, but you haven't said a word so far, Vadim. What is your opinion of Astrug? What's he like as a lecturer?'

'It's hard for me to say. He's only been teaching us for six months. An optional course on Dostoyevsky . . .'

'That's exactly what I meant!' Yulia Mikhailovna announced with a certain triumph. 'An indecisive assessment says a great deal. Only six months! But six months is a long time. Sonya, you're always biased about people and you like to overestimate.'

'What do I like to overestimate?'

'You like to overestimate unpleasant things and injustices. Why should there not be a *single* particle of truth in the criticism of Boris? Is he an ideal, infallible man without any failings at all? I think he has faults, and not little ones either. To be frank, I think he has some rather big faults.'

When Yulia Mikhailovna grew nervous or excited, certain gaps in her command of Russian became noticeable. It was still correct; she made neither grammatical nor lexical mistakes, but a barely detectable loss of accuracy crept in. As she became more nervous, she began to describe Astrug's short-comings: he was unable to make people like him; he had made no impression in six months. She herself taught, and she knew for certain – she was prepared to have a bet on it – that she could win the attention and sympathy of a lecture hall of young people in two hours of teaching. She needed no longer than that, and they would be coming to see her at home, ringing her up and giving her flowers at holidays. After two hours!

As she said this, Yulia Mikhailovna put her arms akimbo and gave her husband and Glebov a slightly patronising look. What she had said was indeed no more than the plain truth. The students loved her. Then Yulia Mikhailovna mentioned another of Astrug's failings: he liked to brag and show off his knowledge. Both he and his wife Vera – especially she – were occasionally prone to give themselves airs. They had a high opinion of themselves. Now what cause had they, one might ask, to put on airs and graces in front of Ganchuk? It looked ridiculous. Now, of course, one felt sorry for them. Without a decent job he could easily go downhill and fade away. And she would fade away, too, without the chance of queening it among the staff wives.

Smiling gently and sympathetically, Sonya listened to her mother in the way that grown-ups listen to the chattering of children. Nikolai Vasilievich did not want to continue the argument. Turning to Anikeyev, who was standing in the doorway and impatiently jingling the car keys, he said, 'Ivan Grigorievich, you at least don't put on airs, do you? Sit down and have some tea . . .'

But Yulia Mikhailovna was determined to have the last word. 'No, my friends, we must take a broader view. The fact is, they were hoping to get rid of Ganchuk. Boris Astrug, unfortunately, is vulnerable to criticism and therefore represents an ideal target; that is also a fact.'

'Nonetheless, I will intervene in this affair,' said Nikolai Vasilievich briskly. 'And that's that!'

In the car, Yulia sat in front beside Anikeyev; Glebov and Sonya sat in the back, between them a bundle of dirty laundry wrapped in a tablecloth. Yulia Mikhailovna kept up a ceaseless flow of stories and comments about matters at the institute, which were extremely involved and of which Ganchuk had no conception; she, however, understood them only too well. The principal didn't like Ganchuk – Yulia always called her husband 'Ganchuk', both to his face and behind his back – because Ganchuk was independent; he was

74

too great a figure to be ordered about, and Dorodnov, the director of studies, was a nonentity who would never forget that Ganchuk had refused to support him in his dubious manoeuvrings over his doctoral dissertation. And that wasn't all. They had old scores to settle. They were hoping to unseat Ganchuk as head of his department – but just let them try! It wouldn't be so easy: Ganchuk was, after all, an old Communist who had fought in the Civil War, author of a hundred and eighty published works, translated into eight European and seven Asiatic languages. And Boris Astrug, his pupil, was a very convenient tool with which to . . . Glebov and Sonya listened to Yulia Mikhailovna with less than complete attention. They were occupied with each other. All the way they caressed each other with their fingers, he with his right hand and she with her left. With his left hand he kept hold of the bundle of laundry. Glebov saw that Sonya's cheeks were glowing and heard her voice tremble very slightly when she said now and again: 'Yes, Mama . . . Of course, Mama . . . You're right.'

'All the same, Sonya, I would prefer Ganchuk to resign from the institute . . . Well? What do you think of that idea?' Yulia Mikhailovna turned unexpectedly round and seemed to see something in Sonya's expression that surprised her. She turned round again and was silent.

Sonya said nothing to her in reply then, but just as they were approaching Moscow, she said, 'No doubt you're right, Mama. But Papa will never leave of his own accord.'

That night at the *dacha* when everything had happened, when the melting snow had dripped and it was too stuffy to breathe . . . Sonya saw it all in her mind's eye as she sat in the car. Glebov remembered it even now, twenty-five years later, although it would have been better to forget it. Then there were other nights, despite the fact that it was January, exams were looming and there was a sudden, violently cold spell that made it difficult to move about. They took the train out to Bruskovo, because no one would disturb them there, and it was allegedly a more convenient place to study for exams. Running through the frostbound woods, they burst into the *dacha*; it was icy cold, but in two hours they had warmed it up. Glebov kept thinking that surely her parents had guessed what was going on? They were, after all, preparing for different exams at different times. What they were doing was really absurd: rushing out of town, spending two hours on the way and then sitting around in an otherwise empty house revising different subjects. They told her parents that several of their friends went out there with them. It was unbelievable that they didn't notice how Sonya had changed. Yet they noticed nothing. Sonya asserted firmly that they hadn't guessed.

Even when Sonya failed some test and laughed when she told about it – it was unusual for her both to have failed and to laugh about it – neither her father nor her mother were put on their guard. They were unshakably convinced that Sonya would pass, and with top marks. It was in her genes, like her pale complexion. And in this they were right. They knew their daughter well. She even passed in the subjects that she managed to read up only on the morning before the exam, because examination candidates usually revise at night and Glebov and Sonya were otherwise occupied at night. Quite a few gaps were left in the work that Glebov was supposed to be doing, too, but he considered that what happened between him and Sonya during that January was his chief exam, immeasurably more important than anything else.

The first to find out was Vasyona – her thin, bony, yellow face reminded Glebov of medieval engravings of Death with a scythe – and it was she who took a swipe at Glebov, as though with a scythe. One day she said to Sonya, when she knew that Glebov was standing within earshot: 'That fancy man of yours never wipes his feet when he comes in . . . behaves as if he's in some bar . . .'

'What was that, Vasyona?' Glebov asked, going up to her. 'And what does "fancy man" mean?'

'How do I know? It's just a word people use . . .' grumbled Vasyona.

Turning even paler than usual, Sonya embraced the old woman. 'Vasyona dear, why do you talk like that? You're good and kind . . .'

At the end of January, Sonya told Glebov there had been a calamity: her mother had unexpectedly driven out to the *dacha* with Anikeyev to collect some things and had found certain unmistakable evidence that they had carelessly left lying around in their hurry to catch the train back into town. Although she used to blame Ganchuk for being naïve and unable to see what was going on under his nose, Sonya's mother was, if anything, even more naïve and had a habit of mentally brushing aside anything that distressed her. It was an unconscious reflex, like an ostrich putting its head in the sand, and on this occasion it resulted in an imaginative interpretation of what she had seen:

'Sonya, I have something unpleasant to tell you. Strangers broke into the *dacha* and spent the night there. They didn't take anything; they just came and slept there.'

'Really?' said Sonya, terrified.

'Yes, unfortunately it's true. They left behind some rather nasty traces to prove it. I won't tell your father, because there's no point in upsetting him when there's nothing to be done about it.'

After some thought, Glebov said, 'What if Yulia Mikhailovna is perfectly well aware of what's happening and was obliquely letting us know this?'

He saw no great harm in it. They didn't have to keep it an absolute secret: they had, after all, decided to get married; nothing could alter that and it was just a question of time – now, in six months, in a year, what difference did it make?

He believed this sincerely because it seemed absolutely firm and final and it could never be otherwise. They grew closer all the time. He couldn't spend a day without her. Now, when so many years have passed since that winter, it was possible to analyse it calmly: What had it been? True love that had matured slowly and naturally, or the physical infatuation of youth which had suddenly struck them like a disease? Probably the latter. Something blind, unthinking and heedless and so unlike his usual self. Another point was that she, too, turned out to be quite unlike the girl he had grown used to in those earlier years. Her taciturnity, shyness and anaemic appearance – all that was left behind in the distant past. And only her kindness and submissiveness remained.

I remember the pain he caused me and how I still went on liking him. He would phone up, in the morning – Father and Mother knew who was calling and made a point of not picking up the receiver because I got angry when they did that – and I would rush headlong from wherever I might be at that moment: in the kitchen, where I was finishing a plateful of disgusting, sticky, lumpy semolina; in the bathroom, and

77

even in the place from which, as I heard the phone ring through the door, I would rush out with my fly buttons still undone. 'Hello!' I would shout. 'Who's speaking?' I wanted to hear his name. He never gave his name, but always thought up something witty or absurd: 'Sir,' he would say, 'I shall await you at eight-fifteen precisely under the clock in the central courtyard, and kindly come wearing your sword. I shall skewer you like a rabbit. You will make a splendid joint of roast meat, sir!' 'And you, sir,' I shouted, breathless with happy laughter, 'you, sir, will make some very good meat balls! Yes indeed, sir! Juicy, tasty, fried meat balls, sir!'

It was awful – I could only copy him. Nothing original came into my head, and if it did, then only much later. I was at the meeting place five minutes early and waited for him, dying with impatience. In all my long life I cannot remember ever having waited for anyone with such trembling and such an agonising fear of being let down, because Anton Ovchinnikov, as befits a true scholar and a great man, was incredibly absent-minded, forgetful and unreliable. Having made some arrangement with me, he was quite capable of immediately making a different arrangement with Walrus or Chemist, and I would suddenly see him calmly walking across the other side of the courtyard, heading for the other gateway and paying no attention to me whatsoever, just as if I didn't exist. As if he hadn't just called me and ordered me in conspiratorial tones to meet him under the clock.

When this happened the first time, I threw myself at him in fury: 'What does this mean, sir? I was standing there like a fool, waiting for you, and you walk through the other gate.' He looked at me with what seemed cold contempt and said, 'My dear fellow, did we ever agree that I should go to that particular place? I am entitled to cross the courtyard by any way I choose and with whatever companions I may choose, while it is your business to observe my movements and, if you so wish, to join me precisely at the agreed time . . .' He rapped out this high-flown nonsense in a dry tone that brooked no objection; Walrus and Chemist giggled, and I was reduced to silence. I lacked the skill to argue with him, and I lacked the will to be angry with him. Hanging my head, I slouched along behind him. Chemist, thin as a rake, and fat, podgy Walrus walked along on either side of the stocky Anton Ovchinnikov; despite the frost, he was, of course bareheaded, his flaxen hair flapping, and he wore shorts and gaiters, the bare white gaps between gaiters and shorts tinged with blue; passers-by grinned as they turned to stare at him. He was telling some endless story as Walrus and Chemist listened, open-mouthed.

That winter he developed an enthusiasm for paleaontology. He acquired several large albums in which he drew dinosaurs and pterodactyls and told everyone all he knew about them. I could find nothing better to do than develop an interest in the same thing. I too started an album. I also tried to draw, or rather copy, or, to be more exact, to trace all kinds of antediluvian monsters from books, but the results were so bad and I ruined the books by cutting out the illustrations. I was the one to whom he should have been talking about dinosaurs; yet he wasted his energy on trying to enlighten Walrus and Chemist, who were both, to be quite truthful, a couple of 'crap-eaters'. Anton and I gave the name 'crap-eater' to anyone who limited his knowledge to what was in the school syllabus, and those who got top marks were called 'super crap-eaters'. These were absolutely hopeless cases, mostly girls, but some of them were boys – two or three miserable shrimps. There were not many 'octopuses' – this was our name for those pure and honourable devotees of knowledge who were interested in all sorts of things, regardless of whether they were taught in school. There was Anton Ovchinnikov, perhaps myself and one or two others; the only female octopus was Sonya Ganchuk, who studied mystic literature, such as the stories of Edgar Allan Poe. Besides, Sonya's father had a most splendid library – at least as good as Captain Nemo's library – and we often went to Sonya's to find out information.

It was Anton who conceived a marvellous idea – to create the SSTW, the Secret Society for Testing the Will. This happened after a gang beat us up in Deryugin Street. When Anton had recovered, we decided to go there again. The group consisted of Anton, Chemist, Walrus, Lev Shulepa and myself, but there at once arose the problem of Vadim Glebov, nicknamed French Loaf, who lived in Deryugin Street. Should we invite him to join the secret society? Once long ago he had brought to school a long French loaf of bread, which he ate in class and shared with those who wanted some. And there were plenty who did. It seemed like nothing special: he simply brought a French loaf, which anyone could buy at a bakery for fifteen kopecks; but only he, and no one else, thought of doing it. During break everyone asked him for a piece and he doled it out to them like Christ feeding the five thousand. However, he didn't give it to everyone; he refused to give it to some people – those, for instance, who brought cheese or salami sandwiches to school, and who wanted a hunk of fresh bread just as much as anyone else. For a long time Vadim Glebov interested me as a somewhat enigmatic personality. For some reason, many people wanted to be friends with him. He seemed to fit in with everybody: he was like this and he was like that; he got on with this crowd and that crowd; he wasn't bad and he wasn't good; he wasn't very selfish and he wasn't very generous; he was not exactly an *octopus* and not quite a *crap-eater* either; he was no coward, yet not noticeably brave; he didn't seem sly or cunning, yet at the same time he was not a simpleton. He could be friends with both Lev and Manyunya, though Lev and Manyunya couldn't stand each other. He was on good terms with Anton, was invited home by both Chemist and Lev, while managing to keep on the right side of the Deryugin Street gang, who hated us; he was simultaneously friends with Anton Ovchinnikov and Minka Bychkov.

So we were faced with a problem: how should we treat him? Should we tell him our secret? Lev Shulepa stood up for him warmly; he said that French Loaf would never give us away. Anton, too, was inclined to accept French Loaf into the SSTW, because he might be useful. I don't remember all the arguments and discussions – I only remember that the chief pleasure lay in the fact that we were deciding someone's fate. Would he suit us or not? I do remember, though, that the decision about French Loaf worried me particularly. I very much didn't want him to join our secret society, but I could not bring myself to say this aloud or to explain my reasons for it. And this was because a girl was mixed up in it. Well, of course that was the real reason. Sonya Ganchuk was in love with French Loaf, this insignificant, colourless creature who was neither one thing nor another. What did she see in him? His ears stuck out, half his face was covered in freckles, he had gaps between his teeth, and his walk was an ungainly shamble; his hair was dark and shiny, combed over to one side, and so slick that he looked as if he had just climbed out of the river and brushed it down. I never could understand what attracted her to him, but the fact was obvious to everyone: she blushed when she talked to him, tried to stay in the classroom whenever he was class monitor, asked him stupid questions and laughed when he tried to make a joke. He was one of those people who can't tell jokes; his attempts at humour had more sarcasm than wit. For instance, he was fond of sneering at Yarik, and would make spiteful remarks about him. Oh, what the hell – maybe I imagined all this simply because he annoyed me. The fact was that even Yarik had a soft spot for him and wanted to be friends with him . . .

The thing about Vadim Glebov was that he was a *nothing person*. Later, I realised that to be a *nothing person* is a rare gift. People who have the ability to be *nothing* to the point of genius always go far. The whole essence lies in the fact that anyone who comes into contact with them projects onto that background of *nothingness* whatever is suggested to them by their own desires and fears. *Nothing people* are always lucky. In my lifetime I have come across two or three others of that remarkable breed – I only recalled French Loaf Glebov because he was the first to reap such obvious rewards for effectively doing *nothing* – and I was always surprised at the way they were carried onwards and upwards by the kindness of fate. After all, in his particular sphere even Vadim French Loaf became a big wheel, although I don't know exactly what it was, because it was of no interest to me; but whenever someone talked about him and his successes, I wasn't surprised: that was how fate meant it to be. And in those days – it seems like a century ago – when five little boys were trying to settle the burning problem of whether or not to initiate him into our secret, he was, of course, lucky as usual. We decided to tell him the secret and accept him. Anton said the war with the Deryugin Street gang would be a long one, a war of attrition, and we needed to have our man in their camp. So one day after school we took Vadim to a secluded spot and told him all about it. He had already suspected something and was obviously thrilled to be asked to join the SSTW. But his answer . . . Oh, it was a most remarkable answer! At the time we didn't appreciate it properly, but years later it suddenly came to one in a flash of comprehension: that was a classic example of the power of the *nothing* personality.

He said he would be glad to join the SSTW, but he wanted

the right to leave it whenever it suited him. In other words, he wanted to belong to our society and simultaneously not belong to it. After a while, we tumbled to the extraordinary advantage of adopting this position: he knew our secret, while not being wholly with us. By the time we had grasped this, it was already too late. We were in his hands. I remember that we planned another march down Deryugin Street and named the day, but Vadim said the day was unsuitable and we should postpone it for a week – then another week, then for three days, refusing, with an air of great mystery, to give his reasons, and we agreed, because he was one of us, though not completely, and at any moment he might drop out of the game. 'If you want to, do it today, but without me . . .' We began to fear he would warn Minka Bychkov, and the whole plan of a sudden raid on the street would collapse. Our aim was simply to walk up and down Deryugin Street, where the resident gang had previously injured and robbed the kids from our house, and if they attacked us, to fight back. Lev Shulepa promised to bring his German pistol that fired blanks and made a bang as loud as a real revolver.

At last French Loaf said: 'Today's the day'. We set off at five o'clock in the afternoon. As we approached the Deryugin house, we saw French Loaf's pale face at the first-floor window; he saw us too, and waved. We walked down the whole length of the street and no one attacked us. No black dog appeared. There were some kids tobogganing down a mound of packed snow in the middle of the roadway, but they paid us no attention. We stopped at the gateway into one yard, and at another, but still no pirates showed up – neither Minka or Taranka Bychkov, no one. Shulepa fired into the air, we waited a little longer and then went home. Everyone was disappointed. No testing of our will had taken place. We went there a couple more times, still without any results. What had happened? Where had they all gone? We never did find out, or maybe I have forgotten after all these years. I can remember nothing except a feeling of annoyance and a strange hunch that Vadim Glebov had fixed it all, to our displeasure and to his own advantage . . .

Later there were various ordeals, fears, nocturnal expeditions to the crypt and underground passages beneath our little local church. And the balcony of Sonya's flat over the abyss. That balcony. And the deathly cold that gripped our hands.

And Sonya's face, white, with that mad stare. Four of us were left. French Loaf refused to say yes or no right up to the last moment, and the fat Walrus backed out in an agony of shame – he suffered from dizziness. We had to choose the most suitable flat. Chemist's place was no good, because his flat was full of people and we would never be sure of being alone on the balcony. Lev's flat was also swarming with people – relatives, hangers-on – and Lev's mother tended to stay indoors for days on end. Anton lived on the ground floor, and I lived on the second floor. There remained the poor invalid Walrus. His home was ideal: on the seventh floor, with a mother who was away at work all day and a deaf old maid who could be locked in the kitchen if one gave her a copy of *Pioneers' Pravda* to read. The old woman loved reading this children's newspaper. Walrus, however, suddenly objected. He objected in general to this particular ordeal, saying that it wasn't a test of will but a test of health. It was then that I remembered Sonya. To be honest, I never forgot about her for a moment.

Sonya lived on the eighth floor, and her parents happened to be away just then. The maid was at home, but she went out at times and Sonya was alone in the flat for hours on end. The eighth floor: it was, of course, incredibly attractive. Exactly what was wanted. The higher the better, the tougher the ordeal. We agreed on this, although our stomachs were churning with fear. The only thing that worried Anton was that a girl had been initiated into the secret; he was categorically opposed to women: 'I haven't even told my mother about this, and normally I tell her everything.'

It was true that Anton's mother was always right up to date with his plans and projects. If you called her up and asked what Anton was doing, she would reply: 'Just now he's finishing the third part of his album of paleaontology. Flying lizards. And he's already halfway with his Italian album. It's turned out very well, especially Vesuvius . . .'

Oh God, how I longed for Sonya to be present at this latest test of will. I suggested we could conceal from her what we were going to do by saying that we octopuses had to go and talk in secret on the balcony and ask her to stay in her father's study for an half hour. If she gave her word of honour as an octopus that she wouldn't leave the study, then she wouldn't upset our plan. Anton hummed and hawed, but finally agreed: 'All right. Sonya, of course, is at least different from other girls because she understands Verdi. She even sang the Grand March from *Aïda* once, although admittedly with a few mistakes.' Coming from Anton, this was praise indeed. Mankind was divided into those who understood Verdi and those who didn't; the former were the best people, the latter were an ignorant rabble. A day was chosen, and we went up to Sonya's place. I can't say that we went bravely and willingly. My legs felt slightly weak, and ants seemed to be running up and down the bones inside them. None of the other members of the secret society looked much better either. I very much wanted French Loaf to funk it at the last moment and not to come; he had the right not to come, and we wouldn't have said anything – but he came, damn him. His face had a greenish tinge, like a corpse. Chemist kept giggling stupidly and trying to make inappropriate jokes.

We planned it to look as if we had come to consult one of the encyclopaedias in Professor Ganchuk's library; suddenly Anton said to Sonya: 'Sonya, you must swear an oath here and now that you . . .'

Disconcerted by all this mystery, Sonya suspected that something funny was going on. She began nervously to try and worm it out of us; 'What are you up to? Why does it have to be on the balcony, of all places? Are you planning to throw someone off?' She had no idea how close she was to the truth. That 'someone' might be any one of us. As I heard Sonya's half-joking questions, I felt tears of self-pity start to my eyes; fortunately no one noticed them.

As I took a few steps around the room I felt my knees trembling and my feet quivering as they trod the ground. Suddenly my legs became a serious cause for alarm. With legs in this state there would be no question of climbing over the parapet of the balcony and around the railings at the height of the eighth floor. I looked furtively at the others. When we each went to the lavatory in turn, I noticed that they were all walking rather unsteadily. Only Anton Ovchinnikov didn't go to the lavatory.

He remained sitting on the chair where he had sat down on arriving, without moving, until the moment came to get up – no sooner and no later. He was short, stocky, broad-shouldered, with a yellowish face and high, prominent cheekbones that made him look like Buddha. When Sonya finally went into the study and locked the door behind her – as Anton had demanded – he was the first to get up and stride firmly into the next room, divided off by heavy curtains and from which a glass door opened on to the balcony. We followed him. The door to the balcony was not locked and not yet taped up for the winter, although the frosty weather had already started. Sonya's father used the balcony every morning to do his exercises. As everywhere else in the block, the balcony was divided in two by a set of iron railings, the other half belonging to the neighbours – and here lay a source of danger: at any moment somebody from the next-door flat might come out onto the balcony and – oh miracle! – save us.

Nobody came out, however, and there was not the slightest sign of life behind the neighbours' window. As I stared at the railings, at the jars, jugs and saucepans standing along the wall and at the curtained glass door, I thought: 'Why don't you look out, just for a second, damn you? It's so easy to hop over the railings and rob your flat . . . What idiotic carelessness on your part . . .'

No, the neighbours were clearly not planning to save us. We were doomed to carry out the test of will. It was about ten degrees outside and we were not wearing coats or caps. My teeth were chattering. Anton went over to the left-hand end of the balcony, where it butted up against the concrete wall, and where the window of the room in which we had just been sitting with Sonya looked out onto the balcony. Anton shook the metal handrail with both hands, using all his strength; it was absolutely secure. Everything was in order. I thought: 'We must all be crazy'. But even if I had wanted to go away at that moment, I couldn't have done it: my legs wouldn't obey me. Down below everything was normal – calm, quiet, snow, black pavements, white courtyards, car roofs – but all of it unattainably far away. We could no more reach the yard below than fly to another planet.

The only way of getting there was to fall.

Anton swung one leg over the parapet, then the other, and slowly moved along it, gripping the handrail with his back turned to the abyss and his face towards us. By this means, moving sideways and very slowly, he reached the next-door balcony and started to come back again, all the while humming a tune; I think it was the Grand March from *Aïda*. We followed him on the other side of the parapet, ready to help him at any moment. I wonder what we could have done? When he reached the wall, he put his bare knee – he was still wearing shorts – on the windowsill, rolled over the handrail on his stomach and fell in a heap at our feet. Immediately after Anton, Chemist set out; he couldn't help showing off, and leaning backwards with outstretched arms he looked down and spat.

At that moment, I saw Sonya's face, twisted into a rigid look of horror, looking out of the window at the end of the balcony.

In a second she was out there with us. Her mouth open soundlessly, she grasped Chemist under the armpits and started to pull him back over the parapet – he told us later that she pulled him with inhuman strength – with her mouth still open as though shouting, but uttering no sound. Chemist tumbled down onto the balcony. We crowded back into the room. We were all frozen, dirty, stained with rust, our faces blue. Sonya seized Vadim Glebov by the hand and wouldn't let him go, afraid that he might pull himself away and climb over the handrail, whispering mechanically: 'Oh, you fools, you fools, you fools . . .' French Loaf frowned with annoyance. He looked offended, as though something had been taken away from him. Later I discovered what had happened. Unable to contain himself, he had secretly blabbed to Sonya – no doubt when he had gone to the lavatory – and advised her to watch the entertaining spectacle. Miserable little sneak. But he saved Lev Shulepa, himself and me. He saved us! My legs were completely useless. People who are neither cowardly nor brave, neither one thing nor the other, sometimes save people who are too much of either. I hated him even more. He snarled at Sonya and said something nasty to her. Then she fainted. We were terrified and called the doctor . . .

And what happened afterwards? Oh, long, long afterwards, you mean? The house emptied. My friends disappeared, all in different directions. Walrus, who had suffered such pangs of shame because he couldn't take part in our tests of will – he couldn't even walk along an ordinary beam in the gymnasium – vanished first of all, probably that same winter. Anyway, we needn't have been in such a hurry to test ourselves: the ordeals came to us soon enough, during the war, and there was no need to invent them. They poured

86

down upon us like heavy rain; some they knocked to the ground, others they soaked to the bone, and some of us perished in that flood. But I do remember this: Anton's mother, Chemist's father and someone else were sitting in our flat, locked in the dining room, where Anton and I were forbidden to enter. However, we listened at the door. Some people's voices can be heard easily, especially when they are talking angrily. I could hear my father saying loudly and angrily: 'Look here – have you consulted a doctor?' And Anton's mother's voice in reply: 'What for?' 'Maybe your son is mentally not quite normal.' Anton's mother laughed, 'My son? What nonsense. My son is quite, quite normal.' Then they all started talking at once, while Anton's mother went on laughing.

That winter, when Glebov's love affair with Sonya began at the *dacha* in Bruskovo, at his home on Deryugin Street the hopelessness that marks all life on the wane thickened into a dense mass. For the life of the Glebov family was fading away: Grandma Nila could hardly walk and could scarcely cope with all the household chores; after his wife's death, Glebov's father had aged and grown bent, eaten away by some disease, and on top of it all he had started to drink. Everything was disintegrating, moving towards the end. Glebov didn't like being at home. His father did not arouse his pity, because this confused, dishevelled old man could not find the courage to accept the end with dignity; instead, he kept hoping for something, dodging and playing sly games with life, dreaming of wheedling from it a few last crumbs of comfort. He also succeeded in wheedling Aunt Paula: after her sister's death she started coming to visit more often, out of family feeling; she helped poor old Nila, and gradually, as though unthinkingly, moved into the place in bed where Glebov's mother had once slept. Where else was she to go? After serving his prison sentence in the far north, Uncle Volodya had left her and gone to Tashkent, where he started a new family. Glebov shrugged it all off. Let them do as they please. He felt a constriction in his chest and the blood thumping in his temples from a premonition of the change that was about to take place in his own life . . .

Aunt Paula had a daughter, however, named Klavdia, who

strongly objected to all this. She would not forgive either her mother or Glebov's father. Aunt Paula's son, Yurka, two years older than Glebov, had died in the war, and Klavdia was married with a baby. She and her husband lived well, and she should have been glad that her mother was no longer lonely and was able to live with Nila and ease her old age, but Klavdia hated her mother. Whenever she came to Deryugin Street, she made it painfully obvious that she had only come to visit Grandma Nila. She hardly said a word to her own mother, and with Glebov's father she was curt and sarcastic.

Klavdia took after her father – she was heavily built, big-boned and ugly. For some reason she was regarded as a good person – it was the same sort of family legend that regarded Aunt Paula as beautiful. Glebov was irritated by the mocking tone in which Klavdia talked to his father, which flustered the old man and made Aunt Paula so nervous that she could only rush about and talk nonsense. With some annoyance Glebov noticed in Klavdia a totally different, alien cast of character, and a nasty streak of cruelty in her nature.

One day she said to Glebov, 'You amaze me: how can you swallow it all so calmly? You seem to have a unique character.'

'In what way?' asked Glebov.

'In the way you accept all this without batting an eyelid. Or maybe it's just a staggering degree of indifference.'

Glebov grinned. 'And what am I supposed to do? I'm a grown-up person, they are grown-up people . . .' He looked at his cousin's face, distorted in a grimace of bitter ill-will, and thought it was better to be indifferent than malicious. Aloud, he said, 'I wish them no harm.'

'My God, who wishes them harm? But it makes me suffer, it's torture to me – yet you don't seem to feel anything. That's what is so extraordinary.'

'I find something else extraordinary: How can you hate your own mother so intensely? Why are you so pitiless?'

Klavdia covered her face with her hands and went out. On a later occasion, however, she confessed to Glebov that she would like to soften her attitude and forgive her mother, but she could not find the strength to do it. Because her mother was the cause of all the family's misfortunes. It had all begun before the war, and got worse during the war. The reason why everything had gone to pieces was that Uncle Volodya hadn't wanted to go on living with Paula and it had broken Glebov's mother's heart. Glebov himself had somehow not noticed any of this, or rather had not understood it. As she told the story, Klavdia suddenly burst into tears and began to curse herself, saying that she was a horrible person, that she shouldn't have said all that to Glebov and begged his forgiveness.

'Now can you understand me, even just a bit?' she said, now weeping, now clutching Glebov by the hand. 'Yes, I am a nasty, bitter, evil-minded woman and I didn't have the right to talk to you like that. What devil gets into me, pig that I am?'

Glebov was amazed, but said calmly, 'Well, what of it? I guessed it myself. I don't blame Aunt Paula.'

'But I do blame her,' Klavdia whispered, and let her head fall to the table. 'I blame her, I do, I do. She deprived me of both mother and father.'

Glebov reflected in silence. Naturally the revelation was painful, but the worst of it had already happened, there was nothing to be done about it, and his only feeling was an increased desire to break away and start everything afresh and on his own.

Sonya began visiting him at home. She wanted to get to know all his family and loved them all even before she met them. Glebov, however, found these visits painful. She saw how pathetic his father was, listened to his futile, ingratiating remarks, saw the poverty, the overcrowding (in his school-days none of this had bothered him at all, friends were constantly coming to see him; but now his own home was becoming more and more of an embarrassment – and in particular he feared Sonya's bewilderment when she faced the most ticklish question of all: who was Aunt Paula and just what was her place in the *ménage*?

Once Sonya turned up when they all happened to be at home, including Klavdia, who had come to visit Nila and had brought some vegetables from the market. It was the end of May and the weather was hot. Glebov introduced Sonya to Klavdia, then quickly took her into his own little cubicle, which was now, thank God, well insulated from the rest of the room in which his father and grandma lived, and where Aunt Paula slept whenever she came to 'help out'. After a half-hour or so, they were invited to drink tea. Glebov was unwilling, but Sonya was eager to see her new friends: this time she particularly wanted to see Klavdia and her four-year-old daughter Svetlana, in whom Sonya was very interested. Sonya and Svetlana liked each other on sight, and at once began chattering and playing some game, which set them apart from the rest of the company. Meanwhile a wearisome family quarrel was in progress, which rarely happened – Klavdia avoided contentious topics in this house. This time the row seemed to break out suddenly, and Klavdia was unable to restrain herself. The cause of the argument was, in fact, little Svetlana, whom her mother wanted taken out of town for a spell of fresh air in the country.

With a disapproving glance at Sonya, who had arrived amid the heat of the argument, Klavdia said in a sharp, quarrelsome voice: 'Now, Mother, give me a definite answer: Will you go with Svetka or not? If not, then I'll make an arrangement with Kolya's aunt, but I don't want to, because she's not well . . .'

Aunt Paula said that the *dacha* they rented was uncomfortable and inconvenient, it was a long way out of town, and she had to go to work in Moscow three times a week. (She was then working for a cooperative, where she wove safety nets that protected workers using machinery.) Anyway, how could she leave Nila without help in the house? At this Klavdia lost her temper: 'Don't use Grandma Nila as an excuse. We'll take her with us to the *dacha*. It'll be even better for her there than here.'

'You don't really think you can drag your granny all the way out there, do you? You must be crazy.'

'Is it so good for her here?'

'She needs the doctors here, you fool! She has to go regularly to the clinic. You're not thinking of her – you only want her as a nanny. She's done enough nannying for one lifetime, thank you very much.'

Grandma Nila objected, saying that she wasn't as sick as all that. Aunt Paula returned to the attack: 'Why don't you put Svetka in a kindergarten? The kindergarten takes all its children out to a *dacha* in the summer. There's a very good kindergarten at your factory, I hear.'

'Who says it's good? You just want to get the child off your hands. Call yourself a grandmother!' said Klavdia in a fury. 'God, the number of times I've vowed never to ask you to do us a favour . . .'

Glebov's father mumbled something; no one could understand what he was muttering through his toothless gums. The women went on quarrelling, not exactly swearing at each other but in an intolerably nasty tone, and, worst of all, totally uninhibited by the presence of Sonya. Klavdia accused her mother of being selfish, saying that she never gave a thought to the little girl and never considered anyone but herself, so what was to be done? If there was no one to go with Svetlana, they would lose their deposit on the *dacha*. Of course, if she had known this in time, she would have fixed her up in a kindergarten, but now it was too late. Aunt Paula said, 'And that's because you never talk to me, your mother. You keep everything to yourself, like the secretive little brute that you are. What harm have I ever done you?' And she burst into tears.

Suddenly Sonya broke in: 'Can I offer you our *dacha*? There is a summerhouse in the garden, which is very comfortable, with electricity and water. Would you like to come to my *dacha*, Svetka?'

'Yes, I would!' cried the little girl, leaping up and down.

Nobody paid any attention to Sonya's remarks, just as if they had not heard them; they simply went on quarrelling. Glebov's father brushed the offer aside with a gesture, and said to Klavdia, 'Don't worry, she'll go; she can quite well manage it.'

Weeping, Aunt Paula shook her head. 'No, I can't go so far out of town. In any case I don't want to go with her; she doesn't want to know me . . .'

Sonya whispered to Glebov, 'Tell them about the *dacha* at Bruskovo. My offer was absolutely serious.'

Klavdia suddenly turned to Sonya: 'Kindly don't interfere in our affairs, young woman. Thanks for the offer, but we couldn't afford your *dacha*. And anyway it is unsuitable.'

'How rude!' said Glebov. 'Come on, Sonya.'

They went back into Glebov's little cubicle and sat down on the bed, covered with a flannelette bedspread. Glebov locked the door and switched on the paper-shaded wall-lamp over the head of the bed. How many evenings and nights had he lain sprawled on this couch under the lampshade, reading and dreaming. He lay down with his shoulders and the back of his head propped against the partition wall – one of his favourite sybaritic poses, which was evident from the greasy mark made by his head on the wallpaper – and Sonya sat alongside him, sinking deep into the sagging middle of the old couch, snuggled up against him with her head on his chest. He embraced her with his left arm, while with his right hand he stroked her thigh, which was encased in a stocking. Above the stocking was an expanse of bare skin. The tedious argument dragged on behind the partition; they could hear every word. Glebov was afraid that Klavdia would say something awful and irreparable, something that Sonya ought not to know. With the palm of his hand he stroked the entirely accessible piece of slightly chilly flesh, which belonged to him, and said that his cousin was arrogant, and uneducated; she had left high school at fifteen and taken some courses at a technical school, and he and she had absolutely nothing in common. She worked as a forewoman in a knitwear factory, and Kolya, her husband, was a machine-fitter in the same factory.

'And I felt sorry for that woman. She's so hard and embittered, it's painful to look at her,' said Sonya. 'And I feel so sorry for your aunt, I think she's a good woman, and beautiful too. The little girl's sweet, but rather weak and not too healthy . . . I'm sorry for all of them, all of them. That's bad, isn't it? I shouldn't feel like that, should I?'

'No, why not? It's a good thing. You *should* feel like that,' said Glebov, continuing to caress the skin through her stocking. Then he unfastened the clip and pushed the stocking down. He could do anything he wanted. She took hold of the fingers of his left hand and pressed them to her lips. The voices behind the partition droned on; this caused him mild irritation; yet over and above it all he felt a great sense of unruffled pleasure – because this woman was submissive, and because she was not just any woman but remarkable, and intelligent with it. He had always suspected that this was the source of her attraction, and now he mentally ordered his hand to derive the utmost possible pleasure from caressing the thigh of an unusual and remarkable woman who belonged wholly to him.

The summer passed, and there began Glebov's fifth and final year at the institute. In the autumn – it was already cold, almost about to snow, probably in November – something happened when Glebov was working flat out on the last stages of his dissertation.

He received a request to report to the dean of studies. The

dean was a man by the name of Druzyaev, recently appointed, whom Glebov hardly knew. He inquired about the progress on the dissertation. Glebov was writing on Russian journalism in the 1880s; it was a vast topic, and he was positively swamped in material, mostly straight quotations amounting to several thousand newspaper pages.

Druzyaev's questions showed that he obviously knew the subject, and he even quoted from memory a little satirical verse of the period, a lampoon on Pobedonostsev, the notoriously reactionary Procurator of the Holy Synod. Perhaps, thought Glebov, Druzyaev had purposely learned it in order to impress him at this interview. Glebov glanced with surprise at this weary-looking man with the telltale signs of heart disease on his flabby face and, as is often the case with heart sufferers, with a kind of dim, hidden melancholy in his eyes, and he wondered why the dean had sent a messenger to the lecture hall to demand his immediate presence. Druzyaev was wearing an officer's tunic and the trousers of an ordinary civilian suit, under which were military boots that squeaked incessantly. All this conveyed a somewhat incongruous impression: the creaking, government-issue boots and the tunic hardly fitted in with the sadness in his eyes and the conversation about liberal editors of the late nineteenth century, spiced by some daringly unorthodox praise for the right-wing journalist Suvorin: 'Just between ourselves, Suvorin was a remarkable character. Enormously talented.'

One fact, however, stuck firmly in Glebov's mind during their talk: until recently Druzyaev had been a military prosecutor, and had been demobilised only a year previously. Another post-graduate student, Shireiko, glanced into the room. He stuck his black-haired, bespectacled head around the door as though just looking in for a second, but on seeing Glebov he decided, for some reason, to come in. He walked over to the dean's desk and sat down in a relaxed and familiar manner as though at home. Glebov took note of this and immediately saw the implications of his obviously close relationship with Druzyaev. At that time Shireiko was making remarkably rapid progress up the academic ladder while still only a post-graduate student. He was lecturing to the final-year students on Gorky, having replaced Astrug. Druzyaev asked Glebov: 'Is Nikolai Vasilievich Ganchuk your supervisor?'

As in the children's game of Hot and Cold, Glebov suddenly sensed that his question was 'warm'. Druzyaev had not said 'Ganchuk', which would have sounded brusque and hostile, nor had he simply said 'Nikolai Vasilievich', which would have been the most natural way to refer to Professor Ganchuk, if not the normal and friendly contraction of name and patronymic into 'Nikvas'; instead, he had chosen to use the precise, official, full version – 'Nikolai Vasilievich Ganchuk' – as though at a prizegiving ceremony or in a funeral announcement. At the same time this form of the name was also respectful, and in some indefinable way it separated the professor in question from the staff as a whole. Did Glebov have full and satisfactory contact with his supervisor? No problems? Glebov confirmed that there were no problems.

It was then that Druzyaev took on a quite different look, a prosecuting attorney's look; his unhealthy appearance seemed to vanish instantaneously, he straightened up and somehow filled out inside his tunic.

'Now, Glebov, the situation is a ticklish one . . . Why did I send for you? I will tell you – only this must remain strictly *entre nous*, as the French say. Shireiko here is fully informed about this little problem of ours.' Druzyaev nodded towards Shireiko, who was listening attentively. 'So don't be surprised that he has joined us. We are all somewhat embarrassed. Did you know that Nikolai Vasilievich Ganchuk had included you in the preliminary list of students who are being recommended for final year post-graduate scholarships? You didn't know? It's news to you? And good news, too, I should imagine. Anyway, apart from that, he is your supervisor. And then in addition you are, as it were, his future, er . . . son-in-law, are you not? Excuse me for mentioning this – my spies have reported it, as they say. And as a military man, I am accustomed to believing the information supplied by intelligence sources.'

Here Druzyaev seemed to unbend slightly; he relaxed, leaned back and even smiled, although the smile was not directed at Glebov but at Shireiko. Glebov mumbled something and shook his head in a vague, noncommittal way, all of which implied that he did not deny the information provided by Druzyaev's 'spies'.

'You see, Glebov,' Druzyaev went on, 'we are not against

your post-graduate scholarship, nor do we have any objection to Ganchuk supervising your dissertation. And of course we cannot possibly object to any future family connection between you and the professor. Nor has it ever worried us – I'm new here, as you know, but my colleagues tell me that this point has already been raised more than once – that Ganchuk's wife, Yulia Mikhailovna, should also be working here in the Modern Languages Department, where she is in charge of the teaching of German. I hope you see where the difficulty lies: each of these things is perfectly admirable in itself, but taken together they add up to rather more than is strictly ethical.'

'In other words, it doesn't look good,' said Shireiko firmly, and added: 'From the point of view of *moralité*.'

Glebov asked, 'Well, what do you propose to do about it?' His attitude was even slightly challenging, because he realised that he was not the target. They explained that it was difficult to talk to the old man; he was accustomed to being above criticism, his old colleagues refused to raise the matter with him, but he must somehow be made aware of the position. Otherwise it would soon be too late; rumours would reach the competent authorities. Would Glebov agree to talk quietly and confidentially to Ganchuk, as a close family friend, and outline the situation to him? Let Ganchuk himself choose another supervisor for Glebov's dissertation; he need only submit his proposal in the usual form, giving whatever reasons he liked. All that was a mere formality, anyway. And that was all the secrets of the Spanish court amounted to. Well then – was comrade Glebov prepared to help them, and in so doing primarily to help himself?

The whole thing seemed perfectly clear and simple to Glebov and he said that he agreed to do as they asked. And on that day there began the chain of deception, confusion and despair that baffled him and finally tore his life into shreds.

If only he had known where it would all lead! But in some things Glebov was a little slow-witted, somewhat lacking in foresight. To him, the complex situation in which he was later embroiled remained a mystery sealed with seven seals. Besides, no one could have foreseen what eventually happened. Druzyaev, himself, for instance, who so audaciously and cunningly started digging his long-distance tunnel under the walls of the mighty fortress, was not to know that in exactly two years he would be flung out of the institute and suffer a stroke, after which he could only sit in a chair by the window, his clawlike hands shaking, and ask his wife in a pathetic whine to light a cigarette for him; and that a further year later Glebov, as a post-graduate student, would read a short announcement in the newspaper: '. . . with profound regret . . . after a grave and prolonged . . .' He heard from others that only eight people turned up at Druzyaev's funeral. Everyone was still disturbed and shattered by Stalin's funeral – it happened in March 1953 – but even that was not the real point. The fact was that Druzyaev vanished as meteorically as he had arisen; and he had arisen, it seemed, simply in order to carry out one short, hard-hitting mission. He had descended on the institute, done his job and disappeared.

For the first few hours, as he reflected on Druzyaev's proposal, Glebov genuinely thought that it was prompted by the new dean's concern for the successful completion of his, Glebov's, dissertation. How naive of him! As far as he could see, it was simply a question of finding a colleague of Ganchuk's who would be prepared to put his signature to work which would actually be done by Nikolai Vasilievich himself, who would thus effectively continue to be Glebov's supervisor. A pure formality, in fact; they were always afraid of trouble caused by formalities.

He decided he would talk to Ganchuk the next day, when he went to see Sonya. The only thought that worried him was something that had not occurred to him at first: how was he to explain to the old man the situation to which Druzyaev had referred so rudely and directly? Although Sonya and he had decided everything, they had said nothing openly to her parents. An unfortunate situation had arisen: to announce this serious decision to Ganchuk simultaneously and in close connection with Druzyaev's proposal would be somehow stupid, and no matter how he might try to phrase such a delicate conversation, Glebov suddenly felt that it would inevitably sound tactless. It would mean artificially accelerating events that ought to develop smoothly, at their natural tempo.

The best thing would be to postpone it; with any luck, the authorities would either forget the whole business or it would somehow sort itself out. It was Glebov's favourite principle: Leave it alone and hope for the best.

Next day he did not go to Sonya, nor for the two following days. He was not purposely avoiding her: his reasons were that he was trying to earn as much money as possible by doing a series of odd jobs, including the most menial kind – chopping firewood with a friend in various Moscow backyards, and at that time of year, just before the onset of winter, there was plenty of such work – but subconsciously he was guided by the wish to put off an awkward encounter in the hope that it would go away. But it refused to go away! After a seminar, Shireiko asked him: 'Have you spoken to him?' Glebov pretended not to understand: 'To whom?' 'To your supervisor. Your future father-in-law.' 'Oh, yes. No, not yet. I haven't spoken to him. There hasn't been an opportunity.' 'Well, please find an opportunity,' said Shireiko coldly. 'We've got to register you somewhere, if not under one supervisor, then under another.'

This Shireiko was only a post-graduate student, yet the things he allowed himself to say! Glebov began to get seriously worried, realising that the mood was exceptionally uncompromising and that leaving it to die a natural death was not going to work. He rang up Sonya. What had happened? Where had he been for the last three days? He explained that he had been working to earn money. She was immediately alarmed: 'You didn't overwork yourself, did you? You're not ill?' That evening Glebov went to see her and told her everything about Druzyaev and Shireiko. It was all too stupid for words – but whose help could he count on in a situation like this? She was dismayed; she could think of nothing to say but 'You must do as you think best'.

It was then that he first noticed that look of hers – a look of total amazement.

'Maybe I shouldn't have told you?' he asked.

'Maybe you shouldn't.' And again she stared at him, smiling and amazed. 'This is a trap. Do you know what I would have said to them if I had been in your place?'

'What?'

'I would have said: "Listen, this is extremely tactless of you. Don't you think it's tactless?" '

'I tried to make them see that,' he lied.

'How did they find out about us? Why do people say such things?' Her voice trembled and tears started to her eyes. Impulsively, he tried to embrace her, but she slipped out of

97

his arms with a quick, agile and uncharacteristically coquettish movement. 'What has happened between us concerns us two, and no one else.'

'Honestly, I was completely thrown off balance . . . I tried to explain,' Glebov muttered, continuing to lie, 'how tactless it all was.'

'You tried to explain? Did you say that it was just idle gossip?' Sonya smiled again. 'I tell you, it's a clever trap. No, Dima, it's all a nightmare. We must not let father's problems mess up our relationship. Mother is having her troubles right now, too: she was called in to see Dorodnov and he said that she had to take some exams, in order to get a Soviet degree and so have the formal right to teach. She has a degree from the University of Vienna. She's been teaching for twenty years. Ridiculous, isn't it?' Sonya took him by the hand. 'Dima, I want to tell you: you are absolutely free. Do as you think you should. And for God's sake don't do anything rash or violent. Do you understand?'

He nodded glumly. At dinner Yulia Mikhailovna, in a state of extreme indignation, described her talk with Dorodnov; how Dorodnov had been courteous and kind, how he pursed his lips into a Cupid's bow, called her 'dear Yulia Mikhailovna' and generally made it all sound as though he had nothing whatever to do with this intrigue, as though certain bureaucrats, faceless and nameless, were demanding that the formalities be observed. Formalities again! Dorodnov was very distressed and constantly apologised. But when Yulia Mikhailovna had remarked that although Sima, the other lecturer in German, had made a précis of the whole of Engels' *Dialectics of Nature*, she still did not know the German language half as well as Yulia Mikhailovna did and never would, Dorodnov suddenly opened his eyes wide in simulated amazement, clasped his hands and said: 'Yulia Mikhailovna, surely you can't be denying the fact that language is a class phenomenon?' Yulia Mikhailovna laughed as she told the story. Ganchuk alternately laughed and frowned. Nothing else but the hilarious news that Yulia Mikhailovna had to take exams was discussed at the dinner table. There was much noise, conjecture and laughter and there were many suggestions; Yulia Mikhailovna revealed a gift for mimicry and gave a comic imitation of Dorodnov, Kunik told them of things that were happening in the

Academy, Yulia Mikhailovna's sister, Elfrieda Mikhailovna – Aunt Elly as Sonya called her, who was quite unlike her sister, a fat, self-confident peroxide blonde – loudly and indignantly denounced bureaucracy. Elfrieda Mikhailovna was a radio journalist. She recalled Lenin's words to the effect that the struggle against bureaucracy would take decades, that the success of this struggle required universal literacy and a universally high standard of education, and that bureaucracy was, of course, a manifestation of the petty-bourgeois spirit, something that should never be forgotten. Whenever Ganchuk was present, Aunt Elly talked in a categorical, didactic tone of voice, as though not he but she were the professor. On the whole, Glebov did not like this woman very much, perhaps because – or so he felt – for some reason she didn't like him. He usually repaid people in their own coin. She was a snob; sometimes she ignored him when he greeted her or merely nodded with arrogant haughtiness. She habitually interrupted him if he said anything at table. Anyway, what did she have to be so conceited about? An unsuccessful journalist, a failed foreign correspondent. It particularly annoyed him that Aunt Elly was regarded as the family hero – because she had spent two weeks in Barcelona as a reporter during the Spanish Civil War. Then she had been recalled. No doubt because she was so stupid. Aunt Elly asked, 'I wonder what your Dorodnov's class origins are? I'm ready to bet they aren't proletarian.'

Yulia Mikhailovna said she didn't know about Dorodnov, but she knew for certain that Druzyaev was the son of a mill owner: '*Voilá*! They spout all these Marxist phrases, but just scratch them and . . .' Ganchuk said they should not flatter themselves: Dorodnov came from a good, working-class background; his father had been an engine driver. '. . . so it's not all so simple as you like to think, my dears.' 'Are you sure you're not mistaken?' Aunt Elly asked obstinately. By the end of dinner they had all cooled off a bit, the comic potential of the Dorodnov episode was exhausted, and Yulia Mikhailovna and Aunt Elly sat down at the piano to play four-handed. Ganchuk and Kunik went off to work in the professor's study.

And Sonya was so unlike her family! She saw everything in a different way from them, and quietly laughed at them. She suddenly whispered to Glebov, 'Do you know what Mama's

and Aunt Elly's father was? The son of a Viennese banker –
although admittedly he was ruined . . .'

She alone, it seemed, had noticed the absurdity in their
ridiculing of Dorodnov, and there was sadness in her smile.

Late that evening, as Glebov came out of Sonya's room, he
walked through the darkened dining room and saw the two
sisters – one slender, with thin legs, the other fat with a big
bottom and a little head, like a traditional tea-cosy in the
shape of a peasant woman – standing by the window, each
with an arm round the other's shoulders and draped with a
single large shawl, looking out at the jewelled mosaic of lights
down below and swaying slightly as they sang together, softly
and beautifully, in German.

I still remember what it was like when we left that house on
the embankment. A wet October day, the smell of mothballs
and dust, the corridor piled high with bundles of books, bags,
trunks, sacks and packages. All this junk had to be brought
downstairs from the fourth floor. Some kids came to help.
Someone asked the lift man: 'Whose is all that junk?' The
man replied: 'Some people from the fourth floor'. He
wouldn't say our name, he didn't nod at me, even though I
was standing right beside him and he knew me perfectly well;
we were just 'some people from the fourth floor'. 'Where are
they going?' 'Who knows? I did hear it was somewhere out of
town.' Again he could have asked me, and I would have told
him, but he didn't ask. As far as he was concerned, I might not
have existed. People who leave that house cease to exist. I
was overcome with shame. I felt it was shameful to have to
display the pathetic innards of our home life out there on the
street, for all to see. All the furniture in the huge flat was
government-issue, so it stayed there. We had sold the piano a
year ago. We had also sold the carpets. But I had grown so
used to those tables and chairs, with their metal inventory-
tags, to those heavy, square armchairs and sofas, covered in
rough material that smelt of disinfectant. I had grown used to
the doors with knobbly frosted glass in their small panels and
to the wallpaper, which, now that the pictures were taken
down (leaving patches of unfaded colour) had taken on an
oddly grubby and naked look. It was still almost ours, yet

already not ours. I hovered indecisively in front of a map of Spain. Should I take it or not? Seven months ago, Madrid had fallen. My passionate concern over the Civil War was ended, the little flags all removed. 'Take it!' said Anton. 'We can still find a use for it.' 'Give it to me,' said Vadim French Loaf, who had shown up without being asked. He followed Anton around wherever he went, like a sucker-fish following a shark. Grandmother came in and said, 'If you don't want to take the map, I'm going to wrap the mincing-machine in it.' No, I'd take it. I pulled out the drawing pins, took down the map and folded it into eight, so that it looked like a fat brochure. I could put it into the pocket of my overcoat. I still have that map to this day among the books in my bookcase. Many years have passed and I have never once unfolded it. But the fact that I absorbed so much suffering and passion – even if they were only childish sufferings and childish passions – could not have just vanished without trace. It must be of some value to someone. At the time, in drizzling rain, standing beside the pile of our junk, waiting for the lorry to come . . .

'What's it like, the flat you're going to?' asked French Loaf.

'I don't know,' I said.

'But I know,' said grandmother. 'It's a very nice place, right alongside a park, lots of greenery, splendid air. True, it will be a long way for me to go to work. First by tram to the city limits, then by bus, about an hour's trip altogether. But fortunately I get on to both the tram and the bus at their terminus stops, so that the seats are empty. We shall be living in one small room in a shared apartment. It's a sunny room, looking out on the yard. A very good room.'

I didn't want to tell any of this to French Loaf. I wasn't in the mood to talk to him. If only he knew how miserable I felt! They had all come running up, fooling around, joking, helping to carry our stuff. They were in an excellent mood; didn't any of them realise that we were probably seeing each other for the last time? It was all right for them – they were staying together. But I was going off to an unknown life, unknown people. Where would I find such friends again – clever ones like Anton, funny ones like Chemist, kind ones like Yarik? And most important of all – where would I find someone else like Sonya? Of course, nowhere on earth. It was pointless even to look or to hope. Naturally there are girls

101

who are maybe prettier than Sonya, who have long plaits, blue eyes and long eyelashes, but none of that matters. Because not one of them can hold a candle to Sonya. The minutes passed, the day grew darker, the lorry would soon arrive and still no sign of Sonya. After all, everyone knew I was leaving today. Why couldn't she show up, if only for a second, if only at a distance to wave goodbye? But she didn't come and didn't come. French Loaf asked, 'How many rooms? Three or four?' 'One,' I said. 'And no lift? Will you have to walk up?' It gave him such pleasure to ask these questions that he couldn't stop himself from grinning.

Suddenly I saw her on the far side of the courtyard, under the concrete archway. Quickly, skirting the black, wet courtyard, she came towards us where we stood outside the door. As she ran up, she asked breathlessly: 'You haven't gone yet? Oh, that's good! There's something for you . . . as a keepsake . . .' and she gave me something wrapped in newspaper, looking as if it might be a book. And she smiled around, not at me, but at everyone.

It was a travelling chess-set, with little holes in the squares to hold the miniature chessmen steady. I had seen others like it in her home. But now nothing pleased me. We were leaving – for a lifetime, forever! Why didn't they realise how terrible that was: Forever? I couldn't utter a word, but just looked at her pale, slightly freckled face, saw her smiling with those kind lips, the kindly look of her shortsighted eyes in which there was nothing but cheerfulness, sympathy, warmth – for everyone . . .

'Well, goodbye,' I said, holding out my hand to her. The lorry drove up. People shouted, grandmother fussed around and got annoyed. We threw all our junk into the back of the lorry. Grandmother sat beside the driver, while my sister and I clambered over the tailboard and settled down among the baggage. My sister was pressing our cat, Barsik, to her chest. It was still raining, thank God, so practically no one was there to see us go. Only the lift man in his black peaked cap came out onto the porch and stood there with his hands clasped behind his back, looking not at me and not at my sister but at the truck, nodding his head very slightly: either he was nodding goodbye to us or he was thinking about something and nodding to his own thoughts, or he was glad to see us go. The rain-darkened asphalt courtyard, where I had spent my life until that moment, was rolling away from us. I saw my friends of that vanished life waving their hands. They no longer looked cheerful but they didn't look very sad either, and the girl was smiling at someone. I guessed she was smiling at the person who had been the real reason for her coming to see me off.

It was like the impossible situation symbolised by the knight at the crossroads in the fairy story: go straight on and you will be slain; go to the left and you will lose your horse; go to the right and you will meet some other form of disaster (although in some stories it said: go to the right and you'll find the treasure). Glebov belonged to a special breed of knight: he was prepared to hang around at the crossroads until the last possible moment, until that final split second, when others are prone to fall fainting with exhaustion. He was a knight who could temporise, a knight who could stretch the rubber of patience until the very instant before it snapped; one of those who never decide anything themselves but leave the decisions to their horse. What was it? Was it mental laziness, thoughtlessness combined with a Micawberish hope that 'something would turn up', or was it a hopeless perplexity at life's perennial tendency to place one, day in, day out, at major or minor crossroads? Now that so many years have passed, and one can at last clearly discern all the roads and little pathways radiating out from that dim, distant and forgotten crossroads, there emerges a strange and semi-intelligible pattern, one which no one in those far-off days could have guessed. It is the same process by which ancient cities, long since vanished and buried beneath the dunes, are rediscovered amid the sands of the desert by their contours, visible only from an aeroplane at a great height. Much of our past becomes covered with sand, smothered by the dust of time. But what seemed simple and obvious at the time is now suddenly seen from a new angle of vision; we see the bone-structure of our deeds, their skeletal pattern – and it is a pattern of *fear*. What, in those days, did heedless youth have to fear? Impossible to understand, impossible to explain it; thirty years on, no one can ever dig it all up again. But a skeletal pattern does emerge . . . They *forced* Ganchuk out of the institute. And nothing more. Absolutely nothing more!

But there was also fear – utterly despicable, blind, formless, like a creature born in a dark cellar – fear of making a false move, fear of defying . . . what? Nobody knew. And that fear was embedded so deeply, under such dense layers, that it was hard to believe anything of the sort had ever existed.

At the time it seemed to be just a case of incomprehension, simply a lack of sufficient love, merely unthinking foolishness. During half-time at an ice-hockey match in the stadium, where Glebov had gone to see Lev Shulepnikov (the bastard had carelessly blabbed to people at the institute about Glebov's affair with Sonya, so to make up for it he ought now to help him with some constructive advice), Lev suddenly said spitefully: 'Look – you don't need Ganchuk; he's trouble'. 'Why don't I need him?' But somewhere deep down, semi-consciously, he was already half-guessing at the reason. Of course he didn't need him if Lev said so; through his stepfather, Lev had access to certain kinds of information that never filtered down to ordinary mortals. Shulepnikov rammed it home mercilessly: 'You don't need him because I say so! Listen to me, you idiot. I'm telling you for your own good'. But Glebov stalked away, unwilling to listen.

He had come to see Lev in order to find the answer to something that was worrying him to distraction and seemed more important than anything else: can a person know with certainty whether they are really in love or not? Where other people were concerned, he somehow always knew for sure: yes, he or she is in love; there was never any doubt. But what about oneself? He must find out; it was vitally necessary because he was standing at a crossroads. He sometimes felt that he was genuinely attached to her, that it was really serious and no fooling, that he was miserable if he didn't see her for a day or two, but then at other moments he would suddenly realise that he hadn't once thought of her for a whole evening. Then when he suddenly, as it were, regained his memory and started thinking about her, he felt a start of self-reproach, like a naughty schoolboy: 'What's the matter with me? Why, that's really horrible!' Then at once he could be overwhelmed by an almost passionate desire to see her as soon as possible and he would ring up, make arrangements about where and how they could meet. That winter his friend Pavlik Dembo, who was a lighting technician in a film studio, gave them a key to his apartment in Kharitonovsky Street, so to be together Glebov and Sonya no longer had to go by train all the way out to Bruskovo, which took up so much time and energy. In any case, in that second winter he might actually have lacked the necessary enthusiasm to make constant trips out to Bruskovo. The amount of effort it required was really appalling; it needed almost a whole day, and usually meant spending the night there as well, whereas in Pavlik's apartment it took only a couple of hours. Admittedly it was much better at Bruskovo; there he was not plagued by doubts about the true nature of his feelings. In Pavlik's dark, nasty little room, where it always smelled of food – there was a restaurant underneath and the smells seeped up through the floorboards, and sometimes when the restaurant staff mounted a campaign to exterminate the cockroaches, the place reeked of disinfectant and the flat was threatened with a plague of cockroaches fleeing from destruction – in that grubby bachelor's pad Glebov experienced the first attacks of loss of self-confidence, of inability to understand his own feelings, or, put more simply, of post-coital depression. Suddenly he would develop an aversion to her touch, her caresses, even to her voice; he would turn away in an access of gloom – there was absolutely nothing he could do to fight off the gloom, which gripped him against his will – and he would wonder miserably: 'Can love really vanish just like that, in a second? This must mean that it's not love at all, but something else.' Of course he was being a fool, reacting like a little boy; yet in some important respect, when he was trying to grapple with this vital problem, he was not being a fool. Who has not been tormented by the riddle: Is this true love? Most people try to guess the answer to this in other people, but Glebov obstinately insisted on conducting the inquiry on himself, because although he did not know it from experience he had either guessed it or read about it in some book – there is no more perilous union than one founded on pseudo-love. It would lead to nothing but unhappiness, ruin, or a gradual, tedious descent into a frigid state that was the very negation of life. But how was he to discover the truth about his feelings? He was particularly alarmed by one shameful, intimate fact: in Pavlik's apartment their lovemaking was occasionally not so good as at Bruskovo. There were times when he couldn't come, despite protracted and exhausting efforts. Sonya couldn't understand what was wrong, and almost

105

wept with pity for him. She thought it was her fault, as she always blamed herself for everything: 'You need another woman!' Naturally he hotly denied this, but in his heart of hearts he couldn't help thinking: 'Perhaps I do . . .'

But then, perhaps he didn't! There were other, good times at Kharitonovsky Street. There was never any doubt about her love, her kindness and devotion. At the time, like a fool, he undervalued these gifts. And she had another gift: an inability to conceal either her thoughts, her feelings or the slightest movement of her heart. Oh, she could be devious with other people! But only in order to share with him the pleasure of the most ruthless frankness. One day she told how she and Kunik almost lost their heads – and how she had hurt and offended him. She was eighteen at the time, it was summer in Bruskovo, the war was just over, the train service was frequently interrupted and they were stranded together at the *dacha*. That night there was a thunderstorm, lightning was flashing and thunder cracking all around, several panes of glass were broken on the verandah and rain was falling in torrents. She was so afraid of thunder that she almost went crazy, and in this state of mental turmoil she rushed into Kunik's room. Being partially deaf, he did not hear the thunder and was asleep, but he did his best to calm her down, wrapped her in a blanket, cuddled her, put her to bed on the divan – and in the process went out of his mind with desire for her. Through the fright, which made her shiver as though with freezing cold, she suddenly realised that this man had gone crazy. He was ceaselessly babbling some gibberish about 'Your mother and my mother . . .' She hadn't the strength to lift a finger, let alone shout or scream; the crashing of the thunder had petrified her. He no longer had the strength of will to control himself. He crawled over on all fours, and tried to climb up onto the divan from the floor. He seemed to be moving like someone in a nightmare, when every movement requires a colossal effort. When he was lying alongside her and put his arms around her, she pushed him away, he fell to the floor and silently crawled back like a beaten dog. Her agony was indescribable – it was what you feel after you have punched someone in the face. What made it worse was that he was such a kind, weak person who was so close to her family and whose only fault was that he had momentarily lost his head. She agonised, not knowing what to do, how to smooth

106

over this awful episode. And what must *he* have been feeling! Out of pity for him and from her own pangs of conscience she was prepared to do anything. But of course next morning nothing was said about the previous night, as though it had never been.

'Why don't you say something?' asked Sonya, and she began kissing Glebov. He was silent because he was slightly shattered by the story, but not so much as to admit it. 'And what should I do? Challenge him to a duel?' Suddenly, and as though through a smile, she quietly began to cry: 'No, no! Never, don't do any such thing. It's just that I've never told anyone but you.'

To have told him this story – in reality it was a trivial matter, because after all nothing had happened – was for her a heroic feat, a purification. She wanted not a scrap of her life to be hidden from him. In any case, what did she have to hide? Not much had accumulated in her twenty-two years – adolescent friendships, other people's problems, the dubious experiences of her girl friends who came to share them with her and seek her advice. She advised them. But when the real thing overwhelmed her, she kept her mouth shut and said not a word to anyone. Her student friends, who had once been drawn to her house, to the fun and parties, to the generosity and the cakes from the special Academy shop, had now all disappeared from her life. She no longer needed any of them – and not out of hardness, jealousy or selfish greed but simply because her whole being was filled by him and there was no room for anyone else. How could such a girl be made unhappy? She was threatened by something terrible: unrequited love . . .

But above this cluster of painful dilemmas there secretly hovered – invisible at the time, though now its outlines are clear – a nasty little skeleton called *fear*. For that, if nothing else, was genuine, even though one realised it only much later. The decades pass; and when everything has long since been hushed up and buried, and there is no way of understanding it all except by exhumation, no one will undertake that hellish piece of spade work. Then, grey as slate, suddenly from the darkness steps the skeleton.

Glebov was told: 'You will come on Thursday and speak at a meeting.'

After an instant's thought, he was just starting to make up

some lie about someone at home being sick when he was interrupted by three words: '*more than essential*'. He then realised that he had made a mistake; he shouldn't have tried to get out of it on the grounds of family sickness, because if the matter was '*more than essential*' the institute authorities would take measures to ensure his attendance: they would contact relatives, or engage a nurse, and then if some real ailment suddenly happened to strike, say, on Wednesday . . . But there was nothing to be done about it now. He said that he would certainly come, although he did not believe for a moment that he would. It was really quite out of the question. 'You must not only attend – you must also speak,' was the firm amendment to the original summons. 'Repeat briefly what you said to us. You will not be required to make any general statement or express an opinion. Just a few factual details, but these are vital. Without them, the business won't hold together . . .'

That sentence drove itself into Glebov's mind like a nail. For hours he pondered on it, repeating it mentally with the same intonation that Druzyaev had used, trying to work out whether this was a threat or a statement of fact, whether the words applied to him, to Ganchuk or to the administration. Whose 'business' wouldn't 'hold together'? Several days previously, when talking to Druzyaev and Shireiko (these two were the prime movers in the plot to oust Ganchuk; the other lecturers submitted unwillingly or were even secretly opposed to it), Glebov had let slip a remark about the wretched little plaster busts that stood on top of the bookcase in Ganchuk's study. Druzyaev said in a kindly tone, with a charming smile, 'Vadim, please describe Nikolai Vasilievich's study, if you can. What books does he have, what pictures, what photographs are there on the walls?' The question implied a kind of verbal police-search of the room, rather as someone else might request a verbal portrait. He decided not to mention certain books and pictures that he remembered, such as a photograph of Ganchuk in the Civil War taken with the now proscribed poet Demyan Bedny, both of them wearing pointed cloth-covered 'Budyonny' helmets, and an inscribed photograph of Solomon Lozovsky, a trade-union leader of the 1920s; although Lozovsky was still in official favour, Glebov nevertheless showed a prescient caution. He had merely mentioned the little plaster busts, standing like a row of toy soldiers just below the ceiling, half-jokingly, as a minor detail. Shireiko, however, at once assumed a stern look and asked in a grating voice: 'Which are the philosophers that Professor Ganchuk keeps on his bookshelf?'

Glebov could not remember them all. He recalled Plato, Aristotle, and, he thought, Kant and Schopenhauer and possibly one other German. 'And what about the materialist philosophers? Do you remember if any of them are included?' Glebov thought hard, trying to remember. He believed Spinoza was there, but he wasn't sure. 'Ah, Spinoza! Of course,' said Shireiko. 'But Spinoza was not a true materialist. And what about the materialists of antiquity – Democritus, Heraclitus? Perhaps some of the French encyclopaedists? And Hegel? Ludwig Feuerbach?' Glebov had already realised that it was a stupid mistake to have mentioned the plaster busts; God knows what idiotic conclusions they might draw from this, so he insisted he couldn't really remember who they were. Then they asked him about the supervision of his dissertation, what advice he was given, what sort of comments or recommendations he received. Did Ganchuk's methodology perhaps contain any traces of past political unorthodoxy? In particular, for example, the influence of Pereverzev? Glebov firmly dismissed the idea, but his inquisitors persisted. An insufficient awareness of the significance of the class struggle? Overemphasis on the subconscious? Camouflaged Menshevism? He fought hard to ward off all these accusations, aware that once they made even one of them stick both he and the professor would be in trouble. Unfortunately, when a person is fiercely intent on hearing a particular *something*, it is hard not to acquiesce even slightly, not to admit to just a particle of that *something*: 'Glebov, you are contradicting yourself. Just now you said . . .' 'Well, perhaps in some small degree . . . minimally . . . I didn't give it any significance . . .'

As he was saying goodbye to Glebov, Druzyaev asked him half-jokingly, with a smile – throughout the interview he had alternately frowned like a prosecuting counsel or smiled and chuckled, whereas Shireiko, never letting up for a second, had bored into Glebov with a steely stare – if he would, just for fun, find out the exact names of the philosophers on Ganchuk's bookcase. Glebov promised to do so, thinking to himself: 'What nonsense! Idiocy of the first order. What on earth do they think they can make out of a row of little plaster busts? Whatever they're up to, they must be desperate if they have to stoop to such *fuflo*.' ('*Fuflo*' was a word he had learned from Pavlik Dembo; it was racecourse slang meaning rubbish or nonsense.) Suddenly Shireiko said in a harsh voice: 'I beg to disagree with you, Vikenty Vladimirovich. This is not meant to be done "for fun" but in the cause of truth, in order to discover who are Ganchuk's real idols. This is not just idle curiosity but a matter of real significance.' And Druzyaev, the dean of studies, instantly changed his tune and squirmed in front of this mere assistant lecturer: 'No, no! Of course not, Yury Severianich. I fully share your point of view . . .'

Glebov turned cold as he listened to this revealing little exchange, and at the same time he felt an awful desire to laugh. 'Idols'! All this solemn talk and about sheer trivia. Why, no one had so much as dusted them for twenty years, these 'idols'. They just sat there, a row of ornaments on the top shelf, and no one knew or cared who they were. Very well, if they were really so interested, he would find out.

That evening he joined the Ganchuks for tea. In an unconcerned voice the old man asked whether it was true, as he had heard in the rector's office earlier in the day, that he, Glebov, wanted to change his supervisor?

'What? What?' Yulia Mikhailovna broke in with amazement. 'Dima wants to change his supervisor? He doesn't want *you* any longer? That is remarkable!' And she laughed.

'I thought it was amusing too.'

'Well, he's certainly chosen the right time.'

'Yes, he couldn't have chosen a better time. By the way, an article by Shireiko is appearing on Saturday or Sunday. You don't know him; he's one of our post-graduate students, a rogue. The title of his article is "Lack of Principle Elevated to a Principle". My people have told me. Across all six columns of the bottom half of the front page.'

'Who is it about?' With a look of horror on her face, Yulia Mikhailovna covered her mouth with her hand.

'Well, it's not only about me, but I am the chief figure in it, apparently. The queen on the chessboard. Of course it is a caricature, distorted out of recognition, but what is particularly disgusting is that I am made out to be lacking in principles.'

'Oh my God . . .' groaned Yulia Mikhailovna.

Very pale, Sonya stared questioningly at Glebov, but Glebov had frozen, unable to move or utter a word.

'I don't know the details, because I haven't read it yet. There's something in it about persistent traces of Menshevism, which surprised me, because as it so happens I have fought against Menshevism all my life. That is one obvious error; he should have taken the trouble to make even a cursory study of my biography. But on the whole . . .'

'Why don't you say something, Dima?' shrieked Yulia Mikhailovna, banging her fist on the table.

'I don't know . . . Sonya had better tell you . . .' Glebov muttered as he got up from the table. He went out, almost at a run, to Sonya's room.

Sonya was not long in coming. He was pacing the room from corner to corner, from one bookcase to the other, smoking furiously, cursing himself for not having had it out with Ganchuk sooner, and cursing Druzyaev. That was a really mean trick – to tell it prematurely to the unsuspecting Ganchuk. They had obviously done it on purpose, in order to force Glebov into making the decision and simultaneously to ruin his relationship with Ganchuk. What if he were to cock a snook at Druzyaev and refuse to change his supervisor? Who would support him, whom could he rely on? What right had they to put this pressure on him?

Sonya ran into the room and rushed over to him.

'Dima! You look terrible!' Impulsively, she put her hand on his shoulder. It was such a comradely, schoolgirlish gesture of encouragement. 'How do you feel? You're pale. I've told them everything, absolutely everything . . .' She looked at him with alarm. He was startled by her appearance, her lifeless pallor, and by the trembling of the hand on his shoulder. 'Papa understood at once. Mama didn't understand at first, but then she understood too and said, "Well, perhaps he's right . . ." '

'And did you tell them about, you know . . . about us?'

'Yes. I told them everything. Including the talk we had about this horrible trap, when you came and asked my advice and I couldn't – no, I wouldn't – give you any advice . . .'

Then Ganchuk appeared, purple in the face and looking somewhat perplexed. 'I understand and I forgive you . . .

111

anyhow, what am I saying – understanding means forgiving. But in future you might remember to mention such things in good time.'

He embraced Glebov and patted him on the back. Sonya wiped her eyes. All three were worried and keyed-up, but each in a different way. Ganchuk proposed that they should all drink a glass of Kagor; he always kept a bottle of this cloyingly sweet drink in the sideboard. He used to say that his grandfather, his mother's father, a country priest had been very fond of this wine, known as 'church wine', and had bequeathed this predilection to his daughter, so that Kagor reminded him of his childhood in a remote village in Chernigov province – the smell of a commode, the feel of rough pinewood floors, cows mooing in the evening – and although Glebov could not stand the muck, he naturally agreed.

They went back into the big dining room, told Yulia Mikhailovna, who was noisily clearing away the tea table (Vasyona went to bed early, and the evening meals were served without her), that they all wanted to drink a glass of Kagor, to which Yulia Mikhailovna, without interrupting her housewifely chore, replied that she had a very bad *Kopfschmerz*. After this she carried out a tray full of dirty crockery and did not come back. She did not once look at Glebov, and her behaviour was generally rather strange, as though Sonya had told her nothing.

Ganchuk explained to Glebov – to whom he now showed the confidence due to a member of the family – the reasons why this campaign had been mounted against him. No one had expected such a turn of events. There was, of course, a pretext: he had defended Astrug, Rodichevsky and certain others who had been criticised in an impermissible manner. When people were being undeservedly humiliated, he could not stand aside and be silent. And Dorodnov – one must bear in mind that he was the prime mover in this whole affair, the rest were just pulleys and cogwheels – had been hoping that he, Ganchuk, would maintain an aloof, Olympian silence. And he was an Olympian – a corresponding member of the Academy of Sciences. But his restraint had snapped. Incidentally, that was part of their plan too: to provoke him. Yes, he had pitched in – he had written letters, taken the matter to higher authority. In a word, war . . . What else could he have done? Boris Astrug had been his pupil, Rodichevsky was a man of enormous talent . . . He had not hoped to reinstate them in their jobs, neither of them would return to the institute, but at least he wanted the smear removed from their names: excessive veneration of Western scholarship and culture, rootless cosmopolitanism – a particularly disgusting and hypocritical cover for anti-Semitism – and God knows what else, a whole ragbag of fabricated nonsense. Boris Astrug had served as a front-line officer through the whole war and earned several medals; yet they had the effrontery to accuse him of 'excessive veneration of the West'! Well, Astrug had made a few mistakes in his time – there were some methodological lapses in his book on Gorky – but what of it? Who didn't commit a few methodological errors? Dorodnov himself, for instance, had piled up a whole heap of blunders in his book on romanticism, and what's more the book was worthless. Nothing but other people's ideas, cooked up together to make it look like original work. But none of the people who had been hounded out of their jobs were ideologically hostile; they were not enemies. He, Ganchuk, knew what it meant to strike down enemies. His hand had never trembled when the revolution had ordered him to shoot. In Chernigov, before he had gone away to study, he had served in a 'special detachment' of the *Cheka*. In those days, the name of Ganchuk had struck fear into the hearts of the enemies of the revolution. Because he had never shown any hesitation or pity. When one day his own father, who was then a very sick man, had interceded to save the life of a certain priest (he was suspected of being linked with a gang of terrorists), Ganchuk had refused to spare him. The priest was eliminated along with the gang; he was a wolf in sheep's clothing who had the blood of several Red Army soldiers on his conscience. For that Ganchuk had broken with his own father and the quarrel was never made up for the rest of the old man's life. That was how they settled such problems in those days.

'And nowadays? Who is prepared to destroy comrade Dorodnov? The reasons, of course, go a lot deeper. Once again I am amazed at the genius of Marx, who in every phenomenon, every fact of life was able to discern its dialectical and class essence. And it is just that, my dear Dima, that you too must learn if you are going to stand firmly on your own two feet. Back in the twenties, Dorodnov caught it really hot. He was a fellow traveller, naturally not a Party member, and he used to churn out some rubbish in the spirit of those bourgeois writers who tried to come to terms with the Soviet regime – in other words, a typical petty-bourgeois faker, slightly camouflaged under fashionable slogans and attitudes, at a time when all sorts of private and cooperative publishing houses sprang up like mushrooms, little cliques and little magazines with half-baked political ideas, and it was then that we should have smashed Dorodnov. But we didn't. He slunk away out of sight, changed his colours, crawled into the woodwork, as so many of them did, in order to re-emerge now in a new guise. What a joke: *he* tries to teach *me* Marxism! A dropout from school with an old-regime right-wing psychology accuses me of underestimating the role of the class struggle . . . He can thank God he didn't fall into my hands in 1920. I would have smashed him as a counter-revolutionary! That was a cardinal error: we failed to stamp out the petty bourgeoisie. Now that the regime has stood the test of time, the great ordeals are behind us and the hour has come to garner the harvest they have come crawling out of their little holes, in various disguises – the vermin that we failed to exterminate in those days . . . I grant you that they look and sound like super-revolutionaries. They pride themselves on quoting Marx and Lenin wholesale, make themselves out to be the builders of a new world, but their real essence – their stinking bourgeoisness – will always leak out and show through. They grab, scrounge, grow fat, fix themselves up with comfortable jobs, so that they are now in a position to settle old scores with the people who gave them a bashing in the twenties. The swine is hoping to have his revenge. But they're so ignorant and uneducated! They don't understand the simple truth that the bourgeoisie as a class has been liquidated, that there isn't and never will be a place for them on Russian soil. Incidentally, Sonya has told me about a certain important decision. Is it really going to happen? A plan for the revolutionary transformation of the Ganchuk family? In that case we must drink another glass in honour of this great event . . .'

'Yulia! Come here, the young people insist that you join us!' Nikolai Vasilievich called out loudly, excited by the conversation, the wine, and the fact that his wife was

114

exhibiting some sort of vague displeasure.

He could not appreciate what was going on in her mind, if only because Sonya's announcement in itself had not made any particular impression on him. Other matters were tormenting his heated brain: newspaper articles, friends, enemies, the Academy, books, the past. Also old age and the nearness of death. His face, which a short while ago had been blotchy with worried perplexity, was now suffused with an even deep-pink flush brought on by the wine – the colour of the little marzipan apples that people hang on Christmas trees. Yulia Mikhailovna was still laid low with *Kopfschmerz*. Sonya looked happily at Glebov, who took Ganchuk by the arm and led him into the study; the professor wanted to show him an album of photographs taken during the Civil War. 'I'll show you a boy who packed a *very* heavy punch. I wouldn't have advised you – do you hear, Dima – to let that boy catch sight of you in those days. Ah, how he hated learned young men in spectacles. He cut them down straightaway – ha! ha! – without asking who their mama and papa were.'

Glebov remember that he, too, had something to look for in the study – the names on those damned little plaster busts.

'*More than essential*,' Druzyaev had said. '*On Thursday, the day after tomorrow*.' He had also said, in that same conversation – the two remarks were continuous and inseparable, like two different-coloured pieces of Plasticine rolled into a ball between your hands or into one long, soft, sticky sausage, and when you rolled balls of it between your palms you suddenly remembered the weakness and submissiveness of childhood, when other hands took hold of you like a piece of Plasticine and kneaded you, squeezed you, compressed you, flattened you and made what they wanted out of you – he had said, as though by the way, in a subordinate clause of the same sentence as the one in which he had discussed *Thursday*, that a provisional decision had been made about the award of the Griboyedov Scholarship. To him, Glebov. On the results of the winter term. Glebov had not reacted, had kept silent, playing the same game – as though this news, so casually dropped into the conversation, was really insignificant and unworthy of attention – although his whole body had flushed for a moment with a hot thrill. The Griboyedov Scholarship! He would only hold it for his last few months at the institute, but even so, it was a blessing. It at once occurred to him that it was not the extra money that was important but the moral boost – onwards and upwards. The news, however, also contained its dose of poison – the sad realisation came to him a second after his initial excitement – because it was inseparably linked with *Thursday*. It was either both together, or nothing.

'To go and speak against Ganchuk – it's unthinkable!' That evening he went to see Lev Shulepnikov, again with an insane hope – unshaken since childhood – that Lev could work miracles. What could he do? How could he influence them? Glebov imagined that Lev – well, not Lev himself, but his stepfather – only had to say to the institute administration, 'Stop harassing Glebov', and they would immediately back off. How much more of it, he wondered, could he stand? There was a limit to human tolerance. First he was ordered to change his supervisor, then to tell them about Ganchuk's ideological deviations and God knows what else, then name the books in his bookshelves. And he had gone along with this sickening business; he had agreed to it and told them what they wanted to hear. As if that were not enough, they wanted him to speak at the meeting. Wasn't that the last straw?

Lev appeared to listen sympathetically, grinned and nodded while twiddling the knobs of a hitherto unknown piece of apparatus: a television set. In the little whitish window something flickered and twitched vaguely, and singing was heard in snatches – an opera was being transmitted from the Bolshoi Theatre. It was said that there were only seventy-five of these television sets in the whole of Moscow. Obsessed with this new toy, Lev swore at it as the picture suddenly went fuzzy and temporarily disappeared. His mother and aunt had stayed home specially to see this programme, and as a result Glebov could not have the confidential talk with Lev that he had wanted. But this was his only chance, so Glebov had to bring it all out into the open with the two women sitting there. Lev's mother said impulsively:

'Lev, you absolutely must help Dima!'

'Do you think so?'

'Yes, I do. I remember Sonya very well – she's a sweet girl. I don't know her father. But really, how disgraceful – to exploit the feelings of two young people . . .'

'Oh, feelings-schmeelings . . .' Lev dismissed the notion

116

with a flip gesture.

'You, of course, wouldn't know anything about feelings,' said Alina Fyodorovna sarcastically. 'For someone who has no musical ear, all music is noise.'

'Alina, please don't upset yourself,' said her sister.

'Did you come to see an opera on television or did you come to lecture me?' asked Lev.

'What's the use of talking to you!' Alina Fyodorovna gave a sharp wave of her hand, which was exactly the same gesture that her son had just made. After a silence, she whispered to no one in particular: 'Making such a mess of his life – and at his age . . .'

The television screen grew brighter, the figures of singers could be seen on the stage and for a while there was silence while everyone watched the screen and listened to the singing. Lev sat on the floor in front of the set. Turning to Glebov, he said cheerfully: 'The picture will be better. We need a new aerial. Jan is getting me one. Everything depends on the aerial.'

'Lev, I repeat – you must do something for Dima and Sonya!' There was a note of sharp irritation in her voice. Glebov did not like this; he was afraid that she might make Lev lose his temper. There was always some kind of discord between him and his mother. 'Tell me, why can you never do anything for other people? It's mean of you. You really must not be so arrantly selfish. An old friend comes to you and asks you for help . . .'

'But what can I do?' Lev burst out. 'Who am I – the principal? The deputy minister of education?'

'You could do something. We know. You've surrounded yourself with such a gang of scoundrels that you practically . . .'

'Mother, leave my friends out of this – all right?' Lev shook his finger at her, but quite good-naturedly. The whole conversation was somehow unnatural: his mother attacked him more out of habit than from a generous impulse to stand up for Glebov; he listened to her with only half an ear; and both had somehow agreed in advance that the outcome of the contest would be a draw. 'Why are you making such a fuss about it, French Loaf? I don't quite understand.'

Glebov repeated that he merely wished Druzyaev and Company would stop twisting his arm. Couldn't they do their own dirty work without him? Was it really essential to humiliate people to such a degree? 'No, Glebov, you must come to the meeting and say your piece; your opinion is of great value because of all the people in the institute, you are the closest to the professor.' But what would happen afterwards? How could he ever look Sonya in the face again? 'Say your piece!' That was easily said. What hypocrisy! They didn't mean 'Say your piece' – they meant 'smear yourself with shit'. Come to the meeting and pour shit over yourself in public.

'Listen to Miss Purity!' Lev suddenly snapped at him in fury. 'It's all right for other people to get their hands dirty, but I prefer to stand aside – is that it? Is that it? You're a nice one!'

Glebov said that it was easier for others, because they didn't have such close relations with the Ganchuk family. He realised that Lev couldn't, or rather wouldn't, do anything. He shouldn't have come at all. Lev had changed a lot. His mother was right: he had developed an attitude of monstrous indifference to everything. Hence, no doubt, that sudden, inexplicable outburst of animal spite. Something like guilt must lie behind such spite as a reaction to anything mildly unpleasant or inconvenient, such as being asked to ring people up, ask people favours. In an irritated tone Lev continued to hold forth, asserting that there was nothing terrible in going up to the rostrum and saying a few words if one had to. He, too, was going to speak at the meeting, although this embarrassed him because he had known Ganchuk since childhood, and in any case he didn't have the time or the inclination – his mind was occupied with other things. He was in the midst of preparations to make a six-month trip abroad; he was up all night swotting up on English – books and dictionaries were strewn around to prove it. But if they *had* to speak, then there was obviously a good reason for it; the old boy was getting senile anyway; he had long outlived his time but didn't realise it, he was making an undignified fuss instead of bowing out gracefully. Still, there was no point in going through all this oriental ceremonial; it only meant trouble. They ought to know that if you try to sit on a hedgehog like Ganchuk, you get your arse scratched.

When he repeated: 'I shall speak – and I shall put the knife in!' Glebov asked, 'Why?'

'Why?! For his unethical behaviour, for forming cliques.

118

And for being too fond of foreign writers and scholars . . .'

'Rubbish.'

'Why rubbish? I can prove it to you quite easily.'

'Of course you can!' Glebov suddenly yelled at him. 'It's easy enough for you to talk. You're not Sonya Ganchuk's fiancé, God damn you!'

'Are you her fiancé?' Lev gave him a crafty grin, winking with one small, red-rimmed eye. 'I bet you a thousand to one in roubles that you're not. Is it a bet?'

'Lev! What are you saying? You ought to be ashamed of yourself!' said aunt and mother indignantly, without turning away from the television screen, which was still flickering and jerking. While he was talking, Lev now and again leaned forward to twiddle the knobs.

'I'm going,' said Glebov, getting up. 'Goodbye!'

But Lev sprang to his feet and seized Glebov by the arm. 'Wait! Sit down! We'll think up something right away. Know what? Let me ring up Yury Shireiko.'

He went straight to the telephone and called Shireiko. The conversation was amazing: these two were obviously as thick as thieves. Glebov now realised how far Lev had drifted away from him: he no longer knew who his friends were at the institute, let alone in the world at large.

'What are you doing? Burning the midnight oil? Bent over a large-scale map? Still planning the great battle?' Glebov shuddered in advance as he wondered what Lev might say about *him* in that horrible, sneering tone. 'Hey, listen – come over here. We've just got a television set. By special order. Come and watch it. We've just switched it on – there's an opera from the Bolshoi . . . Yes, Dima Glebov's here, your godson. He sends his regards. Thanks, I'll pass it on to him . . . Well, how about it? There's a case of Georgian wine here, *Khvanchkara*; the old man sent it yesterday . . . No? You can't? You can't – or you won't? . . . Listen, there's this little problem – I didn't really want to discuss it with you on the phone, but since you're so busy . . .'

'Don't say anything about me!' whispered Glebov, making negative signals with his hands.

Lev waved him away: sit down and shut up.

'Here's the problem. There's this meeting on Thursday . . . Yes, of course we've read it. Powerful stuff, your article, very powerful.' He winked at Glebov. 'We're sitting here right now, discussing it. It's excellent, right on target. Exactly, exactly. Yes, yes . . . quite right. Exactly.'

Holding the receiver out at arm's length he said through gritted teeth: 'He dreams up all that filth *and* he wants to be complimented on it, the shit! . . . Yes, it is a very successful article. Congratulations. Splendid article. So look, what are we to do about Dima Glebov? It's embarrassing for him to have to speak at the meeting, you understand . . . What? Well, so what? I'm calling you to ask your advice . . .'

Then followed a long and barely intelligible exchange of cryptic remarks, at the end of which Lev flung down the receiver, sighed and announced, 'He doesn't seem very pleased with you. He says no one is forcing you to speak, so you have no reason to make yourself out to be such a sacrificial victim. And he asks why you're running around to everyone and complaining. "He's a whiner, your Glebov" – that's what he said.'

Glebov was too depressed to reply. He'd had a premonition that this phone call would bring nothing but trouble, and he had been right. Lev, on the other hand, was smugly pleased with himself, looking as though he had won the contest and had just dragged Glebov back from the brink of disaster.

'Now you're a free agent: you may speak or not speak – suit yourself. The decision is yours. And I fixed it for you, all right. He respects me, the slimy brute. All they want is for me not to touch them. Now I'll bring in the Khvanchkara. And there's some real *lavash* from the Georgian shop. This is going to be some party.'

Before Glebov had had time to decide whether to go home, to go to Sonya or to stay in this weird household, Lev appeared clutching to his chest four large, dark bottles. The women had already set out the tablecloth, and glasses were tinkling.

There were two days left. Glebov still did not know what he would do on Thursday: both to go and not to go were equally impossible. On Tuesday, after his visit to Lev Shulepnikov, which ended in appalling scenes with everyone blind drunk, he was so utterly knocked out that he simply couldn't get up and go to the institute. He came to his senses at about noon, sprawled across his bed like a corpse – he had staggered home at dawn, senseless, and collapsed as he was, fully dressed –

and when he opened his eyes he saw a doctor in a white coat. The doctor had not come to see him, however, but his grandmother. Old Nila had been badly ill for several days and unable to get up. Through the buzzing and intolerable clatter in his head, as though someone were waving a sheet of corrugated iron by his ear, he heard the doctor talking to his cousin Klavdia. 'And what if you give him an injection?' Klavdia was asking, and her expression was full of hatred. The doctor boomed: 'The decision is yours'. They bared an arm and gave him the injection. As he left the room the doctor, quite young and good-looking with pink cheeks, looked hard at Glebov and said: 'The decision is yours'. Glebov felt a clutching sensation around his heart and the cold wave of a minor heart attack surged through his body. Klavdia sat down beside him, bent her angry white face forward and whispered: 'Grandmother's really bad, I haven't slept for nights, because I've been sitting here looking after her, and you' – there were tears in her eyes – 'turn up like a pig. Where have you been? You've made such a disgusting mess, everything will have to be cleaned . . .'

He felt sorry for Klavdia because she was crying, but he couldn't think of anything to say in explanation, and with an enormous effort all he could do was to croak: 'The decision is yours'. Then fragments of the previous night began to come back to him. What had begun as a respectable domestic evening, with Lev's mother and aunt, a white tablecloth and tinkling wineglasses, had ended up, God knows where, as a hideous binge. In someone's attic flat with semicircular windows, under the eaves. There was an old-fashioned gramophone with a horn. They had to walk along the hallway on tiptoe; someone kept falling down and the others picked him up, roaring with laughter. There was a blonde woman, rather fat, white-skinned with big pores, who kept asking, 'How much do they pay for a dissertation?' When they sat down with Lev's aunt and mother at the round table and drank Khvanchkara, Lev suddenly and very quickly became drunk. Glebov wondered, with some surprise, why he was getting smashed so quickly.

His mother drank glass after glass. Their faces grew more and more alike, so that it became strikingly obvious that they were mother and son. Her little round, birdlike eyes reddened and glittered, and Lev's eyes, already red-rimmed, flashed like sparks. And they quarrelled, punching each other with their knuckles. Lev roared, 'What right do you have to talk like that? What are you? You're nothing but a witch!' Alina Fyodorovna nodded with great dignity and said, 'Yes, I'm a witch. And I'm proud of being a witch.' Her sister agreed: 'Yes, she's a witch, it runs in the family'. Being a witch was regarded as almost a virtue. At any rate, both women hinted that it implied belonging to some kind of élite. We are witches and you are scum.

Glebov knew that he shouldn't have got involved with Lev Shulepa again. Things were bound to get noisy, or a fight would start, or somebody would do something monstrously stupid. It always happened that way. 'Oh, so I'm just scum, am I? And what, may I ask, are you?' Then there was someone called Avdotyin, wearing an army-style tunic, who was also sitting at the table and drinking Khvanchkara. He had a long, droopy, despondent face like a cow's udder. He muttered: 'Everyone pays for himself!' For some reason this phrase stuck in Glebov's memory. There were eight bottles of Khvanchkara. He wanted to get up and go, but his legs wouldn't obey him and he could not stand up. 'If I'm a nonentity, then I'm going to leave them,' Lev said to Glebov. 'What do I want with a couple of witches? Even if she is my mother, I don't want her. To hell with them all – I'm going!'

Avdotyin would not let him go, so Lev punched him in the face. Then Lev and Glebov took off. Some car drove them through the dead of night. They lost their way and couldn't find the right house, while the driver swore at them and wanted to throw them out on to the street. But in the end they got there. It was here that there was the old gramophone with a horn. What did they talk about? How did the row start? Oh, yes, that was it: he tried to persuade Glebov to leave Sonya. 'Sonya's all right, but why do you need to marry her? Don't be an idiot.' And then he said, 'Why don't you just be friends with her? That's perfectly honourable. I'm friends with her, too, and I will be for the rest of my life. Tell her everything, ask her advice. That would be perfect – to have a woman who was a friend . . .'

By now, Glebov realised that Lev was right: it would be perfect to have a woman who was a friend. But Lev's vitality and drive seemed so irresistible, so shattering. Do you need a woman? In the middle of the night? To console you, caress you, say tender, heart-warming things to you – and not for money, but just out of infinite feminine generosity – when you're unhappy, lying in the gutter, and your own mother curses you? Nothing can be so consoling as a woman in the middle of the night. The blonde with the white porous skin, who babbled such nonsense, could offer him only an unreal and intangible sort of happiness – like the bottle of beer which Pomrachinsky was suddenly holding, a man who never drank beer, and whom Glebov bumped into as he crawled around half dead in the corridor, and the beer had been bought by Pomrachinsky's wife to wash her hair with – but even the blonde woman failed to induce total forgetfulness. Because he was unceasingly tormented by the painful thought: What would he do on Thursday?

The affair grew more and more complicated. Ganchuk's supporters – and there were still plenty of them in the institute, including such aces as Professor Kruglov, Simonyan the lecturer in linguistics, and some others, now forgotten, together with various undergraduate and post-graduate students – were getting ready for Thursday, burning with the desire to defend Ganchuk. Not all of them, however, were allowed to speak at the meeting. It was to be an expanded session of the Academic Board, to which the active members of various student associations were to be invited. Glebov was supposed to attend as the vice-chairman of the Student Academic Society. The notification came in an official blue envelope: 'Your attendance is obligatory . . .' On Tuesday evening he was approached by Marina Krasnikova, one of the activists of the Society, a loud girl in a perpetual state of excitement as though mildly intoxicated: her passion for student politics was somewhat excessive. Whatever became of her? This fat girl showed all the signs of heading straight for the Academy of Sciences, or perhaps the Committee of Soviet Women. In fact, she sank without a trace, like a stone dropping to the bottom of a pond . . .

'You must speak on behalf of the Student Academic Society, because Lisakovich is ill,' Marine twittered. 'Here are some points that you should make. Lisakovich dictated them to me over the phone.'

'And what's the matter with Lisakovich? What's he ill with?' said Glebov suspiciously. It seemed that Fedya Lisakovich had cunningly forestalled Glebov, forcing him to attend. Lisakovich was chairman of the SAS. Marina said that he had quinsy, with a high temperature, but he was keen to attend, and hoped to be better by Thursday. The doctor had categorically forbidden it. Glebov asked dubiously what his temperature was. Marina said it was apparently around 101 degrees. The points to make were as follows: Ganchuk was the founder of the Student Academic Society; all the best things that the Society had achieved were due to Ganchuk; Ganchuk's errors were typical of the majority of the staff, so if Ganchuk were removed, all the rest should be fired too. His merits and the services he had rendered far outweighed his mistakes. Not a word to be said about Shireiko's newspaper article. If it couldn't be avoided, then say that it was insufficiently concrete and unconvincing. Assert firmly that we should be proud that Nikolai Vasilievich worked here.

As he read this, Glebov was surprised: Fedya Lisakovich was showing real bravery. One of two things: either he was brave to the point of folly by speaking out so strongly against Druzyaev, Dorodnov and the rest of them, or he knew something. It was turning into a really serious battle. Marina said that Professor Vasily Kruglov, the folklore specialist, a good and much respected old man, had been driven to fury by Shireiko's article and was threatening to resign from the institute if the persecution of Ganchuk didn't cease. 'Well, let him resign,' thought Glebov, putting himself in Druzyaev's place. 'He can't frighten us. No one here is indispensable.' A girl post-graduate student had met Shireiko in the courtyard and when the latter had said good morning to her she had demonstratively turned her back on him. Apparently Shireiko went red in the face and asked loudly: 'What does this mean?' She said nothing and walked away. And almost all the first-year students, for whom he ran a seminar, had failed to turn up to his last class.

Marina Krasnikova had never come to see Glebov at home before. Her arrival signified that passions were at white heat. Marina's eyes burned with noble sympathy for all honourable men and with joy that she too was a member of an honourable society. 'You must speak out! You must speak for all of us. It's a disgrace if students can't defend their own professor.' This onslaught, those flashing eyes and wagging finger reminded Glebov of Druzyaev's 'more than essential'. In effect it was one and the same thing, the same use of terror.

Marina seemed not to notice that there was a very sick woman in the house, a nurse with a black bag, the place reeking of medicines, and Klavdia was pacing up and down the corridor with a tear-stained face. And when Glebov, after some hesitation, nevertheless managed to say, 'You see, my position is rather difficult. My grandmother is sick and we don't know what may happen from one hour to the next . . .' which was a weak and almost hopeless attempt to wriggle out of the net, Marina at once said, 'You can count on me. I'll sit here for an hour, two hours, a whole day, as long as you like. But you *must* attend . . .'

That evening someone else came – Kuno Ivanovich. This visit was quite astounding. Glebov's relations wtih Kuno were distant, and the latter had never been to Glebov's flat before. Whenever Glebov was present, Kuno Ivanovich became infected with a strange form of nervousness: he would get excited, make sarcastic jokes and his voice would begin to shake. Glebov had once visited Kuno Ivanovich at his flat on Gnezdikovsky Street (Ganchuk had sent him to fetch some papers). Kuno's flat surprised Glebov by its cleanliness, tidiness and a quite unbachelorlike degree of comfort. There were lots of flowers in pots and vases standing on tables, on the window ledge and on shelves, all arranged into a very picturesque total effect. The shelves alternated with photographs and reproductions of pictures; each wall was a carefully thought-out work of art. It was all so refined and museumlike, unmasculine and dubious. While Kunik collected the papers, Glebov sat on a pouffe and gazed around at the room. On the wall between two shelves, on which were some muscular-looking cacti in pots, he saw a large photograph of Sonya. There were lots of other photographs, but Sonya's was somehow significantly enlarged. 'How he must suffer,' thought Glebov sarcastically. He firmly and patiently put up with the tone of nervous, didactic superiority which Kunik always adopted when talking to him as a way of stressing his seniority. Glebov in return stayed resolutely calm.

On that evening, too, seeing the frail figure of this little man in his long overcoat, his head permanently inclined downward and to one side, although Glebov was astonished, he remained calm.

Dispensing with any greeting such as 'good evening', Kunik

at once started talking as though they were continuing a conversation that had only just been interrupted.

'My first condition,' he said as he crossed the threshold, 'is that Nikolai Vasilievich mustn't hear anything about this.'

Condition? What was he babbling about? Glebov gestured to this enigmatic creature to follow him down the corridor. Klavdia happened to be coming towards them at that moment.

'Grandmother's asking if you're at home.'

'You can see I am.'

'You haven't been to see her once all day. She's worried that something may have happened to you.'

'Our grandmother is sick,' Glebov explained to Kunik, who appeared not to hear and went on with his speech:

'Because if he finds out, he'll tear me to pieces. He's so proud and touchy. I hope you understand his character: proud, impetuous, naïve and helpless, all mixed together.' They went into Glebov's room, and Kunik, without taking off his hat and coat and without so much as a glance around him, with the air of a sleepwalker, sat down on what was nearest – Glebov's bed. 'For other people he will fight like a lion, go anywhere, lock horns with literally anyone. That was how he fought for that nonentity Astrug. But he is absolutely incapable of fighting for himself. Wouldn't lift a finger. So it is we, his friends, who must act now . . .'

'What on earth can *we* do, miserable Lilliputians?' thought Glebov.

'I insisted to him: "You must reply to Shireiko immediately. Write a letter to the editor, and make it tough. He must not be allowed to publish such beastliness with impunity". He said he wouldn't dream of doing any such thing. He quoted Pushkin: "If someone spits on the tail of my coat from behind, it is my valet's job to remove the spittle". '

'Of course, one can certainly play the role of valet,' said Glebov. 'I have no objection. But what does that mean in practical terms?'

'I am not calling on you to speak out in the role of a valet but in the role of a friend. In the role of an honest man. The fact that he quoted those particular lines from Pushkin only shows that he doesn't understand what is going on. He thinks someone has spat on his coat-tails from behind, whereas in fact they are armed with spears and mean to run them through

126

his gut. That is what is happening. They are out to finish him off.'

'What do you suggest, Kuno Invanovich? What can we do?'

'What can we do,' muttered Kunik, as he shrugged off his overcoat with its black rabbit-fur collar, which fell back onto the bed with one sleeve lying across the pillow. "I have already taken steps. I have written a letter to the editor – eight typewritten pages. Six other people have signed. And now I'm writing to the authorities. I'm not asking anyone else to sign that letter, because it is too vitriolic and I wouldn't like anyone else to get into trouble. But I have nothing to lose, so I'm not afraid. As for you, dear Dima Glebov . . .' For a moment he stared searchingly at Glebov as though in some doubt, one ginger eyebrow twitching. The effect was slightly comic. 'Forgive me for asking you: Can we regard you as a true friend of Nikolai Vasilievich?'

'Why not?'

'Excuse me, but I want an answer. Please answer me.'

'But of course.'

'Of course. Good. In that case, why are you acting so strangely?'

'Excuse me, I don't understand what you mean.'

'Why don't you raise any objections to the way you are being used in this disgusting campaign of persecution?'

At this Glebov was completely dumbfounded. How was he being *used?* Had he, Glebov, read Shireiko's article? Yes, he had, but cursorily, skipping lines as one does when reading something repellent that you would prefer to throw away. In it, apparently, there was the following sentence: 'It is not by chance that certain final-year students have decided to dispense with the services of Professor Ganchuk as their supervisor'. Kuno Ivanovich explained that in fact there was only one of those 'certain final-year students'. He had at first not even bothered to go over to the institute and look with his own eyes at comrade Glebov's application to change his supervisor. When he had been told Glebov's name by telephone, he could not believe his ears, so he went over and checked it. It was unbelievable.

'But do you know what's behind that?' Glebov shouted, 'No, you don't know anything! You don't know the whole background story.'

'Yes, I know, I know.' Kuno gestured with impatience and

disgust, as though afraid of hearing something unpleasant. 'And even if I didn't know, I could guess. But I'm not interested in the background story. The important fact is that you are being used, yet you remain silent. You haven't said anything, Dima. Why not? How can you keep silent and at the same time go to their house, talk to Nikolai Vasilievich and other members of his family? You must agree that it is somewhat, well, what shall I say, less than morally irreproachable . . .'

Glebov glared sullenly at his inquisitorial visitor. At first he wanted to shout: 'And creeping into a terrified young girl's bed during a thunderstorm – how does that rate on the moral scale?' Then he was seared by a feeling of shame and was ready to do anything, to go to any lengths if only he would make up for what had happened. But he could only mumble: 'I really didn't see that sentence in the article . . .'

'As though the sentence itself mattered! Suppose,' roared Kunik, 'a man was attacked and robbed on the street before your eyes, and the muggers asked you, a passer-by, to lend them your handkerchief so that they could gag their victim . . .'

'Will you be quiet?' Glebov implored him. 'Please talk more quietly; there is a very sick woman on the other side of this partition.'

'No, you listen to me! What are you, may one ask? A chance witness or an accomplice? All right, don't answer; there are reasons, there's a background story . . . We'll allow that . . . But what are you going to do *now*? How will you go on living? Wait and hope for the best, as you've done up to now? There's no time left. On Thursday you will be going to your execution, Dima. I can see, though you haven't the guts to stand up and say: "It's not true! It's an injustice!" So your execution it will be – it's inevitable. Sometimes you can put the rope round your own neck by keeping silent.'

Glebov burst out: 'That's not true! I shall speak on Thursday and I'll say everything!' The pale, gingery-haired little man got up from the bed and threw his long overcoat around his shoulders. He flung back his little crooked head and stared at Glebov, frowning intently, and although he was shorter, he seemed to be looking down on him. He did not say goodbye but flew off down the hallway with his fluttering, lunatic gait and out of the front door. As Glebov shut it behind him, Kuno at once knocked again:

'Dima, my dear fellow, one thing I beg of you . . .' he whispered, his pale, anguished face leaning even more heavily over to one side, 'do as you like, but don't tell the old man a word about any of this. Promise? Nothing about my letters, nothing about our conversation. He must not know!'

Thus inexorably Glebov was drawn ever closer to that agonising crossroads. He could no longer feel his legs beneath him, such were the tension and exhaustion; he might fall at any moment. Where could he find refuge? He was being carried away by a powerful undertow. Although he was apparently standing still, he was being swept along. Only, he still didn't know where. Another day flickered past, equally vague and confusing, full of domestic worries, running to the chemist's, irrelevant conversations. Klavdia was again quarrelling with her mother and weeping in the kitchen. She loved Grandma Nila very much. And so did Glebov.

Who else was there to love, if not old Nila?

He sat beside her, holding the old woman's pale-blue hand, as light as a handkerchief, and told her a story – she had asked for it, like a little girl – while his imminent fate boomed in his head like a tolling bell: that way you will lose your horse, that way your wife – and this way, life itself. He was asked to go to the institute for some kind of discussion with the first-year students. But what was there to discuss? So why go? He didn't go. Then Afonicheva called up, the secretary at the dean's office: 'Glebov, you haven't forgotten, have you? Tomorrow at twelve'. The voice rapid and urgent: she had obviously been given a list of twelve people to drum up by telephone. 'No, I haven't forgotten.'

'Come on time, don't be late.'

'Yes, I'll come.'

He tried to reason calmly: there are four possible variants, let's think them all through. First variant: to go, and speak in Ganchuk's defence. Well, not straight out, but let's say with qualifications, mentioning certain shortcomings, but in general making it be a speech for the defence, even if only in the form suggested by Kunik, namely, by analysing that sentence in Shireiko's article and explaining its provocative intention. What would be the outcome of that variant? It would infuriate the administration. Goodbye to the Griboyedov Scholarship, the post-graduate studentship and all the rest. Because it meant making an unexpected change of front, and they wouldn't forgive that. Ever. It would be regarded as treachery. Their vengeance would be swift and terrible. And since Dorodnov now had all the power in his hands – the principal had been absent for months, somewhere in Korea, or it may have been China, or maybe in hospital – he could do exactly as he pleased. He was determined to settle accounts with Ganchuk. What positive gains would result from that variant? The gratitude of Ganchuk and all his family. Sonya's even more boundless love. A few people, such as Marina Krasnikova, would pump his hand for a full half-minute and contratulate him on an excellent speech, and Kunik would say with a grin: 'You surprised me! I'm delighted for your sake!' And that would be all. After that, a life as a minor clerk God knows where. On Sundays, with him loaded like a mule, they would take the train out to Bruskovo. The losses were crushing, the gains dubious.

Second variant: to go and to criticise Ganchuk. Or, put more simply, to bring up the rear of the mob as they attacked him. Naturally he wouldn't do it aggressively or rudely; he would even speak warmly, sympathetically, with profound regret that he was obliged to admit, etc., etc., finishing with an appeal for moderation and to remember Professor Ganchuk's great services, but . . . exactly the kind of thing that Druzyaev had asked him to say. Something about the pernicious influence of Pereverzev and RAPP – it didn't matter which. A passing reference to the plaster busts. Maybe he might forget the plaster busts altogether, or perhaps just make a gently regretful comment. The main thing would be not to say a word about that little sentence in Shireiko's article, as though it had never been. After all, if he put his hand on his heart and was quite sincere about it, was Nikolai Vasilievich perfect in every respect as a teacher and mentor? Might there not even be a grain or two of justice in those cannonballs that were being hurled at this fortress? Secretly one had to admit it: there was . . . His books were boring. Glebov had never been able to read a single one of them through to the end. To be honest – they were unbearably tedious! People wrote like that twenty years ago, but now something different was needed. They all showed ineradicable traces of vulgarised sociology like a hereditary disease. (But not a word must be said about that; he would only ever admit it to himself, in secret, when confessing to his own conscience.) And the accusation that he ran his department like an autocrat was not so far from the truth either. Lecturers were only appointed with his personal sanction, and post-graduate scholarships were given only with his approval. Nor was he nearly as 'unworldly' as people thought; he was observant and discriminating where people were concerned, and by no means a paragon of impartiality: on the contrary he was highly partial, loving some people and hating others, sometimes for no discernible reason. His tastes appeared old-fashioned, his predilections rooted in the past, in those decades of rebellions, struggles and skirmishes. He was obsessed by certain chimeras whose chimerical nature had long since been obvious to most people, but to which he was as attached as a hungry baby to its mother's nipples. And there were the phenomena of recent years – the purges and terror that had taken place in the years before and immediately after the war – which his mind was simply incapable of accepting. Was Dorodnov capable of it? But none of that really mattered; the whole point was that Nikolai Vasilievich was an absolutely honest and decent man, and to attack him implied an attack, as it were, on the very standard of decency itself, because Dorodnov was one thing and Nikolai Vasilievich Ganchuk was something else. Sometimes ill-informed people would ask: What is the difference between them? They had simply changed places for a time. Both of them were flourishing their swords, the only difference was that one was now showing signs of flagging, and the other one had only recently been given his sword. Therefore to attack one, it might seem, was equivalent to attacking the other, too; they were birds of a feather. But that wasn't so. The two men made different movements, like swimmers in a river: one did the crawl, another did the breaststroke. Oh God, was there really any difference between them after all? They were both swimming in the same river, in the same direction. No, it really came down to one thing – parting with Sonya and her love forever. And that was so irrevocable, such a bitter wound to the heart – to deprive oneself of the love of even one person . . . And that wouldn't be all. He would feel it from all sides: people would revile him, would hold their hands behind their back lest they sully themselves by shaking hands with him. Someone, no doubt, would send him a telegram: 'Congratulations on your Griboyedov award of thirty pieces of silver'. None of that would upset him, because his career would suddenly accelerate so fast that he would fly far, far away; all these people would vanish from his horizon and disappear forever with their sneers, their contempt and the blinkers on their eyes which prevented them from seeing that Ganchuk's goose was already cooked before the meeting took place and that nothing Glebov might say would make any difference to the outcome. To try to save him was like swimming against the current in a flood that carried everything before it. You could thrash away until you were exhausted and still be flung lifeless onto the shingle. For fear is the most intangible and the most secret motive force of human self-consciousness. Steel fingers were already noticeably beginning to push him, and he was ready, firmly and finally ready; yet some invisible force was barring the way. Was it Sonya? Whom he didn't love? And who was the best person he had ever met in his life? No, it wasn't Sonya, but the things that made up Sonya's nature: her warmth, her goodness . . . It was those essential qualities within Sonya which constituted the obstacle and which were an impassable barrier.

Therefore if the first two variants were impossible, there was the third. To go and not to speak, to remain silent. That would please nobody. Both sides would hate him for it. Out of the question! So that left the fourth and last variant. *Not to go at all*. But was that possible? He had been warned that his presence was 'more than essential'. Any excuse, therefore, had to be of positively cosmic significance or the result of some near-fatal accident, such as being run over by a car on his way to the meeting. Or perhaps he might kick a stray dog to make it bite him, necessitating an immediate anti-rabies injection. There were countless possibilities – but all of them absurd. If only the loss of consciousness and the heart attack that had happened two days before, after his night out with Lev Shulepnikov, could happen now; but Druzyaev, a former prosecuting attorney, would undoubtedly set up an investigation and find out that the cause of the attack was alcoholic poisoning. No, it was impossible not to go. And to go was equally impossible. Everything was impossible. Stalemate. Not one piece on the board could move.

It was this dilemma – though briefly, jerkily, in a tired voice and with many pauses for reflection – that he described to Grandma Nila, when she asked him to tell her something about his life.

'I love hearing about what you're doing,' she had said.

Nila herself had never worked in her life. Or rather, she had worked all her life, only at home, in the family. Naturally she understood nothing about his problems, but he told her all the same; he had to talk about something, and he had only one thing on his mind.

Suddenly old Nila herself started to tell him some of her memories of the distant past, which she remembered well and in great detail. One summer Grandpa Nikolai, Glebov's great-great-grandfather, had taken her out to the country. He was a merchant, and the family used to live on the Varvarka, near the Salt Market (they had sold that house before the revolution and moved to Shchipok, across the Moscow River), but in a village in Venevsky District there was a house which Grandpa Nikolai had built for his mother-in-law, who had refused to move to Moscow. As a little girl, Nila used to love driving out to the country in summer. Grandpa Nikolai was not popular in the village, where he was nicknamed 'Mr Skinflint', although to Nila he always seemed kind. On the way out to the village, he would buy her a 'raffia horn', a cone-shaped container made of clean, yellow raffia full of cheap gingerbread, nuts and raisins. The mixture was known as *yeralash*; in the shop they would ask for 'two horns of *yeralash*, please'. All the little village girls would be there, waiting for them, as soon as their carriage drove into the yard, and then Nila would distribute the contents of her cones to them: some nuts for you, some sweets for you, some gingerbread for you. Nila's old great-grandmother loved sugar candy. Grandpa Nikolai had built her a cottage there, although she refused to live in it because it was built like a town house, without a proper porch and with a huge drawing room full of city-style furniture. So Great-Grandmama lived in an ordinary peasant's cottage with her daughter, and the 'proper' house was always empty until Nikolai brought his family there in the summer. He would ask her: 'What shall we bring you from Moscow, *mamasha*?' She would invariably reply: 'Sugar candy, Nikolai Efimovich, if it's not too much trouble'. Of course, they always sent her some for Lent, too, as it was one of the things you were allowed to eat during the

133

Lenten fast; then in summer they would never fail to bring her two slabs of sugar candy – it was sold in slabs in Zaitsev's grocery shop. The slabs were not very big, about the size of the small drawers in a writing desk; the candy was displayed in the shop stacked in two layers, each made up of different colours and flavours – lemon, raspberry, apple, plum, as many flavours as you could wish.

So they sat there telling stories to each other, Glebov and his Grandma Nila, and afterwards everyone had the impression that the old lady was feeling much better. She even felt strong enough to offer Glebov some advice on his problems:

'What can I say to you, Dima?' She looked at him with pity, with tears in her eyes, as though he and not she were dying: 'Don't upset yourself, don't aggravate your heart. If there's nothing to be done about it, then don't think about it. It will all sort itself out, you'll see, and whatever that may be, it will be the right way . . .'

And strange to say he fell asleep that night easily, calmly and free of nagging anxiety. At six o'clock next morning he was suddenly awakened by a low voice, or it may have been by something else, and he heard someone say, 'Our Grandmama Nila has gone . . .'

Klavdia was standing in the doorway, black against the brightly lit hallway. The low voice, which he had taken for a man's voice, was hers. Quietly, for fear of disturbing the neighbours, Aunt Paula was sobbing on the other side of the partition. The sound she made was strange and chilling, like the clucking of a chicken whose neck was being wrung. Glebov's father came in, muttering something about the doctor, a death certificate and the need to go somewhere. So began that Thursday. And Glebov was unable to go anywhere on that day.

I came back to the house on the embankment three years later, in September 1941, three months after the German invasion. College hadn't started yet. The nights were cold, but clear and starlit. I remember those nights; we lived a nocturnal existence. The day was spent rushing hither and thither: working at the riverside docks, at the timber yards, or delivering call-up notices from the district military commandant; in our spare time we learned how to control the pumps on a fire engine, how to unreel a fire hose or operate a street fire hydrant. Although amateurs, we were firemen. At the same time we helped out with any job that came to hand. We unloaded cargoes of ammunition at the docks, and at the timber yards we unloaded logs from goods trains. Everything had to be done in a hurry; we didn't stack the timber in neat piles, but simply threw it off the wagons in untidy heaps. The important thing was to clear the track as quickly as possible. That is what I most remember – the mad haste. And I remember how I strained myself trying to lift those gigantic logs. But our real life began at night, after Levitan's voice on the radio had broadcast an air-raid warning. We did our turns of duty, we blundered around in attics, ran over roofs in search of those hellish incendiary bombs, which we would heroically seize with long tongs and throw off the roof; but above all we breathed the deathly chill of those nights.

They were bright, with a kind of ashen glow. The anti-aircraft guns flashed incessantly all around and deafened us with their noise. I shall never forget that smell of powder smoke above the roofs of Moscow, the clatter of shell splinters falling on sheet iron and the sad smell of burning, coming from somewhere beyond Serpukhovskaya Street . . .

The station house of our fire brigade – its full title was something like 'The Komsomol Youth Company of the Lenin District Fire Brigade' – was on the Yakimanka, over the bridge. The house on the embankment did not belong in our sector, but one day we found ourselves there all the same; I forget what we were doing there, or why we were sent there. On the roof, I remember, I met Anton and three other kids; then we ran down to Sonya Ganchuk's apartment, and Vadim French Loaf was there; it was his last day in Moscow before being evacuated. He had come up to say goodbye; their train was leaving at dawn, but they had to go to the station hours beforehand, because the business of getting on the train was so chaotic. I had already seen off my aunt on one of those trains, and I knew what it was like. French Loaf had grown up a lot; he now spoke in a deep bass voice and had even sprouted a thin black moustache. It appeared that he had not only come to say goodbye to Sonya but to fetch a trunk which she had promised to him. I remember him as he stood in the middle of the kitchen, drinking a cup of tea, while

Sonya cleaned the extremely dusty trunk with a brush, when suddenly the lights went out, we started looking for candles or a torch, and at that moment the air-raid alarm sounded. For the second time that night.

When the lights came on again soon afterwards, I saw Sonya's face wet with tears yet smiling. By then I had almost forgotten about Sonya, and my feelings for Vadim French Loaf were of complete indifference. All that was in some long-distant childhood, whose pain has faded with the years.

I remember something else from that night. An enormous Caucasian dagger was dangling from Anton's belt. He and I were standing on the roof beside the thin metal railings and looking down on the black nocturnal city. There was not a gleam or a flicker of light to be seen down below; everything was murky and indistinguishable except for two pink, quivering wounds in the blackness – a couple of fires burning on the left bank of the Moscow River. The city was endlessly vast. It is difficult to defend something so immeasurable, and there was no way of disguising the river; its shining surface reflected the stars, its bends marked out the districts of the city. It hurt us to think of the city, a living creature that needed help. But how could we help it? There was a moment of paralysing silence. We stood on the edge of an invisible abyss and looked up at the sky, where everything quivered and merged in a gamut of moving colours, tense with the expectation of a change in the city's fate: stars, clouds, barrage balloons, the slanting blades of searchlight beams tirelessly cutting into that fragile universe. And then Anton uttered a murmured remark that surprised me:

'Do you know who I feel sorry for? Our mothers.'

By this he meant that our previous selves no longer existed. A violent break had been made in our lives. Time, like the sky, had broken apart with a deafening crash.

Later, we were waiting on the landing for the lift, in order to take Sonya's sick mother downstairs to the air-raid shelter. French Loaf had just said that I had done well to get out of this house in time. The Germans were aiming at it; the building was surrounded by near misses – on the bridge, on the Kadeshevka. I wasn't sure whether he was paying tribute to my cunning or my good luck, but whichever it was, I sensed an undercurrent of spite in his remark. I said nothing to him in reply, because I was quite indifferent to him. Doors were slamming on every floor. All around there was noise, people shouting to each other, footsteps clattering on the staircase so hard that the stairs shook. Everyone was listening to what was happening in the sky. For the moment, all was quiet above us. Anton said, 'Perhaps it's just a lone plane, some bastard on his own?'

The door of the flat opposite the lift opened, and a man came out, an overcoat thrown over his nightshirt, followed by a woman carrying a fat little girl with long legs. From far away came the banging of anti-aircraft guns. Speaking to no one in particular, the woman said:

'Every damn German should be thrown out of this house.' (This remark was aimed, of course, at Sonya's mother.) Then she looked at her husband and asked, 'That's right, isn't it, Kolya?'

When the lift door opened and Sonya's mother made a move to go into it, the woman adroitly pushed her aside with the little girl's legs and said, 'No, you can wait,' and went into the lift first, followed by her husband and someone else. The lift went down. Professor Ganchuk asked: 'Who are they?'

Sonya said they were the new neighbours, and added hesitantly: 'They're not bad people, but a bit strange.'

Anton and I linked our four hands to make a 'chair', put Sonya's mother on it and carried her downstairs to the cellar. Then we had to go back to the Yakimanka. The anti-aircraft fire was getting nearer and louder. When I ran out of doors, the firing was thundering all around and in the intervals between salvoes one could clearly hear the fragments of exploded shells thumping violently into the asphalt. So amid haste and noise I parted from all of them, without a chance to say goodbye.

No – there was one more meeting. I met Anton for the last time at the end of October, in a bakery on the Polyanka. Winter had suddenly hit us with frost and snow, but Anton, of course, wore neither hat nor coat. He said that in two days' time he and his mother were being evacuated to the Urals, and he asked my advice on what to take with him: his diaries, the science-fiction novel he was writing, or the albums of his drawings? His mother had weak arms, so he was the only one who could carry heavy things. His question struck me as absurd. How could anyone be worrying about albums or novels, when the Germans were at the gates of Moscow?

Anton drew or wrote something every day. A notebook, folded in two, was sticking out of the pocket of his jacket. He said, 'I shall make a note of our meeting in this bakery. And our conversation too. Because it is all of historical importance.'

Many years later I came back to see Anton's mother – she was the only one who returned to live in the house on the embankment, to the same little flat on the ground floor – and she gave me the six notebooks that contained Anton's diary. They were his diaries for the last year before the outbreak of war; for some reason they had remained in the Moscow flat and so had survived. All the rest of Anton Ovchinnikov's work, his albums and his scientific studies, had sunk in the river Iset, when the barge in which they were travelling capsized. Anton and his mother barely escaped with their lives.

Something that Glebov tried particularly hard to forget was what Kuno Ivanovich had said to him when, by an absurd coincidence, they met on the Rozhdestvensky Boulevard, and how he, Glebov, had behaved when he heard it. The times were different by then (it happened only eight years ago), but somehow there was still a nervous, keyed-up feeling in the air which affected them – it might have been on the eve of the so-called 'doctors' plot', or it might have been when he was in the process of moving from the institute to his present job – and on top of it all he had to bump into Kuno Ivanovich on Rozhdestvensky Boulevard. It was in the depth of winter. The central avenue of the boulevard had been swept clear of snow, so that the yellow sand showed through, with deep heaps of snow piled up on either side. Someone fell into a snowdrift. Glebov was not the only person walking there at that moment; that was the trouble – it was all said in front of other people, and Glebov lost control of himself. If the passers-by had not pulled him away, it could have ended very badly, because he was unaware of what he was doing. He almost managed to strangle the little man, after throwing him to the ground and gripping his throat. For the rest of his life he tried to forget about it, and nearly succeeded; his memory almost suppressed it – he could not remember, for instance, what Kuno Ivanovich actually said to him – but it persisted in the form of a faint pain in his chest, like the feeling induced by

138

recalling an escape from some horror in the distant past. Whenever he recollected that little man, which occurred very rarely and for no explicable reason, it made itself felt by nothing more than a slight constriction in his chest.

He also did his best not to remember the look on Yulia Mikhailovna's face when she was walking down the hallway, leaning on a girl's arm, having come out of Druzyaev's office. Glebov felt a moment's confusion, not knowing what to do – whether to nod, to say something, or simply to bow in silence – and in his perplexity he simply froze stock-still. Her face, too, froze into a mask as she went past him. He tried very hard indeed to forget those petrified features, because memory is a net which should not be subjected to too much strain by making it bear heavy loads. All those great cast-iron lumps of horror should be allowed to break the net, fall through and disappear. Otherwise we are obliged to live in a constant state of stress. He did forget her bloodless, frozen face, but not for long; it reappeared whenever he heard some news of her, such as her death. She died soon afterwards, when he was still a post-graduate student. But then, she had suffered from a chronically weak heart. No one could understand why she tried so hard to get her job back. In her condition, it was out of the question for her to work. She couldn't work, couldn't judge others, couldn't make trouble, couldn't seek revenge – she could do nothing but lead a quiet life out at Bruskovo amid the shrubs and the flowerbeds, but she refused to accept such a passive existence, and in any case Bruskovo was taken away from them. She brought her death on herself. He never did know in detail what happened; he only knew that her face suddenly appeared in the institute. All the rest he tried to forget. Such as, for instance, what Ganchuk said at the editorial board when it met to consider an article that had been submitted. Nothing insulting was said, and no one else who heard him understood the implications of his remarks. The old man was so sick as to be almost unrecognisable: something had happened to the right side of his face, which made his speech very indistinct, and no one paid much attention to what he was saying. Although he had been reinstated and his chief enemy, Dorodnov, had been crushed and consigned to oblivion – the last few years had been taken up with this struggle – something important had irrevocably gone, and it was not particularly interesting to listen to an old man who was no longer up to par. No one but Glebov listened to his mumblings, but he caught a note of spite in what Ganchuk was saying. He was both piqued and surprised: apparently those scraggy old muscles still had the ability to contract. All that had to be forgotten, as did that September day in Riga, in an open-air café not far from the central department store, when he had seen Sonya sitting at a nearby table. The times were by then quite different, not even like more recent times, but quite, quite different; he could have safely assumed that no one would recognise him; that nothing that might reach him from the unpleasant past was any longer capable of stirring any emotions; and that it had all peeled off and fallen away. He had once heard that Sonya had been taken to a hospital somewhere out of town; this might have been expected, as she had a bad family history: Yulia Mikhailovna's mother had died in an asylum and Yulia Mikhailovna herself, of course, had never enjoyed the best of health. One of the people who had visited Sonya in hospital said that her illness expressed itself in photophobia and a desire to be in darkness all the time. That, apparently, was all: only fear of the light and a longing for the dark. Then, it seemed, she had got better, although he knew nothing definite. There were no more people left to form a link between him and Sonya; he had lost contact with everyone from those days. Then came that meeting in Riga. He was renting a house near the beach, and had come into town for the day. Marina had dragged him round the shops and suddenly there was Sonya sitting at the next table. Beside her was a tall, strange-looking, big-nosed woman in spectacles, dressed untidily like a tourist in baggy trousers and tennis shoes. Sonya looked at Glebov; it was because he felt her glance that he turned around. At once he made an involuntary movement towards her and said something like 'Sonya!' or 'Hello!' or 'Is that you?' Something warm, expressive of the wave of emotion that overwhelmed him for a second. She had aged and put on weight, half of her hair was grey, but she had kept her ability to turn instantly pale; she paled now, looking frightened; then the woman with the big nose took her by the arm, raised her from her seat and led her away. It stuck in his memory that the shoes the woman was wearing were huge, outsize. Marina asked, 'Do you know those women? Who are they?' He said they were old acquaintances from Moscow, but he couldn't remember their names.

Maybe it wasn't quite like that, because he was trying to forget it. Whatever one didn't remember ceased to exist. None of it had ever happened. There never had been that second, crowded meeting in March, when there was no longer any point in reproaching oneself; he had to go anyway, and even if he didn't speak himself, he was at least obliged to listen to the others. He did, it seems, say something at that meeting, something very brief and of very little significance. It had completely escaped his memory. So what? It no longer mattered. Ganchuk's fate had already been decided. He was to be transferred to an obscure teacher training college outside Moscow, '. . . to strengthen the staff there'. Some people objected, somebody clucked in protest like an angry hen, but that was all uninteresting and now forgotten – *it had never happened*. Or had it? One thing, though, was undoubtedly real: the café in Gorky Street. He remembered that for the rest of his days. That *had* happened. But all the rest, the shouting, the excitement, five hours of idiotic talk with breaks for those who wanted to smoke, Lev's drunken babbling, Shireiko's triumph (he had seemed to be heading for the front ranks, marked out as an up-and-coming big wheel, but somehow his progress went no further than those meetings and there his advancement stopped), all the stupid, incomprehensible fuss that was created around Ganchuk, with stamping of feet and twisting of arms, with tears, heart attacks and rejoicing – all that vanished as though sunk in a swamp. No, it didn't happen; nothing of the sort happened. Glebov was staggering along the street, his head muzzy and heavy, and beside him Lev, who was totally smashed. He had managed to stay on his feet in the meeting, and had still looked pretty good when he was on the rostrum. Lev was muttering: 'We're all bastards, pigs . . .' He had to be helped home, or he might have collapsed on the street. It was then that his downfall began. Several years later, when his life really started to go downhill, his second 'dad', the one who looked like a bewhiskered Ukrainian Cossack, turned out to be not up to his job. The flat went, the car vanished, his mother was left alone but managed by a miracle to cling on to something, and Lev turned into a minor administrator in some soccer club; he travelled with the team from town to town, arranged the hotel bookings, looked after the boots and balls, organised unofficial matches, and he drank, for which he was soon sacked. After that he did God knows what, and when the police picked him up dead drunk on the street he would sometimes say his name was Glebov and give Glebov's address. No doubt he gave other names and addresses as well. The police brought him to Glebov twice. But even that was long in the past, about fourteen years ago. And then the waves closed over his head, and Glebov heard nothing more of him until his sudden reappearance now in the furniture shop, when neither of them had any strength left for sentiment about old times – for anything, in fact, except harsh reality.

But back then, after the March meeting and before the deluge, as they swayed and circled around the Moscow streets, neither had any premonition of what was to come: Lev didn't know that he would soon be on the skids, slithering from side to side, like an empty sledge shooting down an icy hillside, and Glebov didn't know that the time would come when he would try not to remember everything that happened to him in those days, and no doubt he didn't know either that he would come to live a life that *hadn't happened*. And suddenly, through the window of a café on Gorky Street, near Pushkin Square, Glebov saw Ganchuk. He was standing at one of the little tall tables where you drink coffee, and was greedily eating a 'Napoleon' cake, holding it in its paper napkin with all five fingers of his hand. His fleshy face, with its pink folds of skin, expressed pure enjoyment as it moved and twitched like a well-fitting mask, the whole skin from jaw to brow vibrating with pleasure. Ganchuk was so absorbed in the sweetness of the cream and the thin crispness of the strips of pastry that he noticed neither Glebov, who was frozen into immobility in front of the window and for a second stared at Ganchuk in amazement, nor Shulepnikov, swaying on his feet beside him. Yet half an hour ago this man had been destroyed. Later, Glebov often told the story of seeing Ganchuk in the café. Yes, he would say, you might think the old man had plenty on his mind at that moment – this, that and the other, all of it forgotten now – yet there he stood eating a Napoleon with the greatest possible enjoyment.

Other things, too, imprinted themselves on his memory, some with all the nuances, some in great detail, some blurred, such as his first visit to the Ganchuk's after his grandmother's funeral, and after the Academic Board meeting which he had been lucky to avoid, but before the second meeting that took place in March. It was one of those well-meaning but stupid things that he was prone to do. Inwardly he had already made up his mind. The stupid part of it was that he still felt the need for Sonya to give him by some indirect, oblique means, her permission. That is to say, he imagined her saying:

'Yes, you're right, my dear, you should leave me. It will be better that way for me, for you, for papa, for your work and for everyone.'

Of course she wouldn't say any such thing, but he wanted her nevertheless to see him and share his suffering, to realise that there had been no alternative. Somehow he was convinced that she would understand; that was after all her greatest quality – she always understood.

The door was opened by Yulia Mikhailovna. Glebov had the impression that when she saw him, Sonya's mother momentarily and very slightly swayed, and there was a barely detectable pause before she said: 'Oh, it's you. Come in.' He entered. There was something in the atmosphere that he had never felt before. With a casual gesture Yulia Mikhailovna pointed to the coat rack: 'You can hang your things there', as if this were his first time in the house. The message was: The house you used to know doesn't exist any more. 'Sonya will come soon. Please wait in the dining room.' With a similar careless wave of the hand he was shown where to sit – on a little divan alongside the piano. Yulia Mikhailovna went out of the room. He sat there alone, feeling fairly calm although sensing a chill in the air and with a foreboding of painful encounters to come, as though in a dentist's waiting room. This visit, however, was essential; the aching tooth had to be pulled out, and so he was prepared to be patient. One thing puzzled him: why was Yulia Mikhailovna so obviously cold towards him? It was incomprehensible. The March meeting had not yet taken place. Surely she couldn't read his thoughts, when he had himself only just made up his mind? He decided that as soon as Yulia Mikhailovna appeared again he would ask her, with genuine surprise: 'What has happened? Why do you seem to be so angry with me?'

Still Yulia Mikhailovna did not come back. Sonya had not yet returned home. He could hear Yulia Mikhailovna's quick little footsteps pattering down the hall, heard her talking to Vasyona; then the study door was opened, followed by the rumbling of Ganchuk's voice and Yulia Mikhailovna saying: 'That is not what I want!' To this Ganchuk made some inaudible reply, after which there was silence. No one came into the dining room. The door opened noiselessly to admit Maurice the cat, who walked past Glebov without looking at him, as though he were a chair, and stalked across the dining room into Sonya's room. By the time Glebov had been sitting on the divan for about a half-hour, he began to get nervous. What sort of way was this to treat him? What grounds had they for this behaviour? There was none. He had, after all, had a very good reason for not going to the Academic Board meeting – a more than good reason: the death of a close and beloved relative was more important than troubles at the institute. A gradually mounting sense of hostility towards Yulia Mikhailovna rose in him – he had always felt there was something small-minded, egotistical and unpleasant about this woman – and he also began to resent Ganchuk, too, because he always gave in to her. For the first time Glebov experienced a certain malicious pleasure in the thought that these people were being made to suffer a certain degree of unpleasant pressure and even hardship. They couldn't go on forever looking down on others from their ivory tower. It was significant, what's more, that so few people had come to their defence. When Yulia Mikhailovna suddenly came in, she was carrying – no tea, no plate of biscuits, not even an ashtray – a table lamp, and Glebov said to her, with a hint of challenge in his voice:

'You seem to be angry with me for some reason, Yulia Mikhailovna.'

Yulia Mikhailovna gave an odd grin but did not immediately reply. She put the lamp on an occasional table in a corner of the room, plugged it in and switched it on. 'Yes, would you believe it? I am angry with you.'

'But why, Yulia Mikhailovna?'

'I can't explain it briefly. We haven't time for a talk. Sonya will be here in a moment. It's rather dark in here, don't you think? I must put the light on. "*Mehr Licht*", as Goethe said before he died.'

She switched on the chandelier and went out again. It was four o'clock in the afternoon and not particularly dark.

144

Suddenly Yulia Mikhailovna reappeared and firmly shut the door behind her; her eyes were flashing, her movements hurried. She sat down on a chair facing the little divan and fixing Glebov with a piercing look she said rapidly, in a low voice:

'All the same, I'll try and explain before Sonya comes. I'm talking quietly, so that Nikolai Vasilievich won't hear. I didn't want this conversation, but you asked me, so . . . Do you know what I think of you? I hate you. Yes, yes, there's no need to look so surprised . . .'

Then she started to spout a stream of unbelievable nonsense. There was something about how hard it was to understand a person, but that there always came a moment (for some reason she said 'a moment in the night') when people revealed themselves. Then something more about her mother, who had been clairvoyant and able to foretell the future. This, he remembered later, had given him a nasty fright: was she clairvoyant too and had she been able to guess his intention to break with Sonya? But as though in answer to his unspoken question, she said that she lacked her mother's gift; she had no idea of the state of his relationship with Sonya, she did not want to interfere, but it did seem to her . . . It filled her with alarm to think . . . She cursed the day that . . . What an extraordinary rigmarole it all was, what an outpouring of malice, absurdity and madness! Obviously the woman was sick. Sonya had once told him that whenever her mother's blood pressure went up and an attack of stenosis was on the way, funny things were likely to happen to her mind. Feeling an urge to get out of the room, Glebov leapt to his feet and said, 'I'll fetch you some water'.

She seized him by the arm and would not let him go. Her fingers held him in a firm grip of unexpected strength, and he felt a momentary chill of anxiety: only a madwoman, he thought, could show such strength. But Yulia Mikhailovna was not insane; she simply hated Glebov and was in a hurry to tell him the reason. Again, as though reading his thoughts, she said rapidly, 'Don't call anyone, I can explain everything before Sonya comes, and then we'll have some tea. And – do you hear? – I haven't said anything to you . . .'

After that, with the same haste, in a half-whisper, gulping between words, she told him that he was intelligent, but that his intelligence was ice-cold, ungenerous and inhuman, an intelligence that was totally selfish, the intelligence of a man of the past . . . and similar remarks that were close to clinical delirium.

'You don't understand how *bourgeois* you are!'

He had, apparently, simply made use of everything: her house, her *dacha*, her books, her husband and her daughter. What could one say in reply to all this? There was no point in arguing with such an unhappy woman. He got up from the divan and asked, 'May I get you a glass of water?'

'Yes, you may,' she said calmly.

He went into the kitchen, Vasyona gave him a glass, which he filled with boiled water and took back into the dining room. Yulia Mikhailovna was sitting on the same chair and staring in front of her.

'Do you know what I think?' she said slowly, as though coming to her senses, as she took the glass. 'It would be best of all if this conversation remained between ourselves. The best thing would be if you would leave this house . . .'

He asked, 'What have I done wrong?'

'Nothing – so far. You have not yet been able to. But why wait until you do? Go away now . . . I ask you, I implore you.' Indeed, there was entreaty in her look. 'Sonya will never know about our conversation. I swear it. Do you want me to give you money?'

'Money? What are you talking about?'

'But you need money, don't you? You love money, isn't that so? And you don't have any. How much would you like me to give you?' The delirious ramblings started again. 'Tell me quickly, before Sonya comes. Go on, tell me. I'll give it to you and then you can leave immediately . . . No, wait! I'll give you something else.' Here she dropped into a whisper. 'I'll give you an antique ring, with a sapphire. You love bourgeois things, don't you? Gold? Gems?'

'If you are so anxious for me to go,' he said, 'then I won't object . . .'

She waved her hands, whispering, 'Just wait a moment and I'll bring it. I don't need it, and you can make good use of it.'

She ran towards the door of a neighbouring room, which was her bedroom, but fortunately she was stopped by Ganchuk, who was coming in. There followed a strange, obscure, jerky conversation about, of all things, the works of Dostoyevsky. Ganchuk said that he had hitherto underrated

Dostoyevsky, that Gorky had been wrong about Dostoyevsky and it was time to reassess him. He would have a lot more spare time now and he proposed to work on the subject.

Yulia Mikhailovna stared at her husband with sad intensity. He said that the thought that had tormented Dostoyevsky – if man's last refuge is nothing but a dark room full of spiders, then *all is permitted* – had hitherto been interpreted in a wholly simplistic, trivial sense. All such profound problems had, in fact, been distorted into pathetically inadequate form, but the problems themselves were still there and would not go away. Today's Raskolnikovs did not murder old women moneylenders with an axe, but they were faced with the same agonising choice: to cross or not to cross the line. In any case, what was the difference between using an axe and any other method? What was the difference between murder and just giving the victim a slight push, provided that it removed him? After all, Raskolnikov didn't commit murder for the sake of world harmony but simply for his own ends, to save his old mother, to get his sister out of a tight spot, and to secure for himself something or other in this life, whatever it might have been . . .

He was thinking aloud, oblivious to whether anyone was listening to him or understanding him. Suddenly Sonya came in, just as Ganchuk was saying, 'And you, Dima – why did you come here? It is completely inexplicable in terms of formal logic. But perhaps there is a reason of another kind . . .'

'Papa!' Sonya shouted, rushing towards Glebov. 'Don't be horrible to Dima. He's suffered enough already . . .'

She stood in front of Glebov, shielding him as though Ganchuk might throw something at him, but Ganchuk was so absorbed that he neither heard nor saw her.

'Perhaps,' said Ganchuk, 'there is a metaphysical explanation. You remember how Raskolnikov was drawn again and again back to that house . . . No, that's not it.' With a brisk, professional gesture he dismissed his own hypothesis. 'In the novel everything was much clearer and simpler, because there was a state of open social conflict . . . But nowadays people don't fully understand what they are doing. Hence the arguments within themselves . . . they are trying to convince themselves . . . The conflict is *internalised* – that is what is happening.'

'Papa, dear,' said Sonya, 'I beg you!'

'All right, my dear. I'm sorry. Excuse me.' For the first time Ganchuk now looked attentively and understandingly at Glebov. 'And I want you to know that I do not bear him the slightest grudge. Absolutely none at all.'

He went out. A short while later, however, when Glebov had followed Sonya into her room and was lying on the rug-covered couch, as he usually did at moments of tiredness, while she sat beside him and stroked his hair, Ganchuk suddenly put his head around the door and said in his old, familiar voice:

'Do you know what our mistake was? We spared Dorodnov in 1928. We should have finished him off.'

Hearing this reassured Glebov; he realised that Ganchuk hadn't changed, that he was his former self again. So everything that had happened had been right. Glebov spent the night with Sonya. They hardly slept but dozed off just before dawn. Glebov had a dream: in a little round tin box that had once held sweets was a collection of old medals, orders, crosses and badges and he was sorting through them, trying to do it quietly in order not to waken somebody. Later in his life, this dream about the medals and badges recurred more than once. Next morning during breakfast in the kitchen, as he sat looking down on the concrete arc of the bridge with its toy people and its toy cars and the greyish-yellow palace with its cap of snow in the Kremlin across the river, he said he would ring her up after lectures and come again that evening. He never went back to that house again.

All this was what Glebov remembered – partly by exerting his memory, partly by involuntary association – during the night after that day on which he had met Lev Shulepnikov in the furniture shop. One thing, however, puzzled him, and by the time he fell asleep in his study on the first-floor with its window on to the garden he had still not solved the riddle: why had Lev refused to recognise him?

* * *

In April 1974, Glebov travelled by train to Paris for a congress of the IALCE (International Association of Literary Critics and Essayists, in which he belonged to the board of management of the essayists' section), and on the train he met Alina Fyodorovna, Lev's mother. She was also going to Paris at the invitation of her sister, who had left Russia fifty-three years before. Alina Fyodorovna had turned into a grey, bent old woman, but Glebov recognised her at once: the same hook-nosed, terracotta-coloured face, the same sharp, glittering look and the same cigarette between her teeth that he remembered from childhood. She stood for hours in the corridor by the window, smoking. Glebov approached her and reminded her who he was, but the conversation failed to get started. Suddenly, as had happened long ago, he sensed the existence of a wall of haughty superiority that surrounded this woman. What reason could she possibly have for acting like this now, for God's sake? Her world was destroyed, her life had fallen apart, her son had disappeared and she had no wish to talk about him; yet the old lady screwed up her eyes as though looking at Glebov through a lorgnette and asked with aristocratic indifference: 'Oh' really? Essayists' section? Is that interesting?' After Warsaw she had become slightly more talkative, and he learned that she was getting a pension due to her as the widow of her first husband, Prokhorov-Pluhnge, an old Communist who had been posthumously rehabilitated, that she had a nice one-room flat on Peace Avenue, not far from the metro, where she lived alone and had no wish to see anyone – neither her dear son nor her ex-daughter-in-law (who had left Lev eight years ago because no one could bear to live with him), nor her grandson, a seventeen-year-old lout who remembered her only when she was about to visit her relatives in Paris. Then he would become the best grandson in the world and visit her, ostensibly to see how she was; he would also casually give her a little order, which he just happened to have typed out, for a pair of jeans, a belt, a cigarette lighter, a blue denim shirt with sewn-on pockets and a fitted waist (the kind to be worn outside your jeans) – all very efficient and carefully thought out. All her life she had lived for others; now she wanted to live for herself. After Berlin she became even more loquacious and frank: 'They say the Russian nobility has degenerated; I heard that said in Paris. But I tell you the opposite: we are a very tough breed because we have been through everything and we have survived.'

At the station in Paris, Glebov saw another hook-nosed old woman who looked somewhat like Alina Fyodorovna but was frailer and fussier in her behaviour; there was nothing Parisian about her clothes, and she wore a voluminous, old-fashioned cloak. With her were a young man and a girl who twittered around Alina Fyodorovna, speaking half in Russian and half in French. As the crowd surged round them, Glebov stood there for two or three minutes, expecting Alina Fyodorovna to look round and say goodbye to him. But Alina Fyodorovna did not so much as glance in Glebov's direction. Instead he heard an insinuating voice say in broken Russian: 'Welcome to Paris, Monsieur Gleboff! Let me take your luggage. Is this all?' The young, tanned, red-cheeked, wet-lipped young man with a thin moustache, named Séculot, whom Glebov remembered from the congresses in Oslo and Zagreb, picked up Glebov's only suitcase, nodded, pointed somewhere with his left hand and led Glebov away through the crowd.

The familiar smell of a Paris station, a heady, bittersweet fusion of aromas, enveloped Glebov like humid air on a hot day. Forty minutes later he was darting briskly back and forth in his rather gloomy hotel room, which looked out onto a narrow street not far from the Place Pigalle. Humming under his breath, he unpacked his suitcase, slammed the wardrobe doors, and almost ran into the bathroom, where he laid out his washing and shaving things under the mirror.

When I was working on a book about the 1920s, I came across the name of Nikolai Vasilievich Ganchuk, who had played a notable part in the discussions of those days, especially in the noisy arguments that had raged around the journal *Literary Outlook* in 1925 and 1926. Someone told me that Ganchuk was still alive. With considerable difficulty I managed to find him. He was living alone in a tiny one-room flat jammed full of books – there were even bookcases in the kitchen – in a new, slab-like block of flats near the Riverboat Station. He had voluntarily given up his old flat (which as a boy I had visited, though he had of course forgotten this and I remembered it only vaguely) because he had not felt able to go on living there alone after Sonya's death. His new place, he assured me, had an excellent climate, the air was made fragrant by the surrounding pine forest and it was a good place to go skiing. He was eighty-six years old. He had shrunk, he stooped and his head had sunk between his shoulders, but his cheekbones still glowed with healthy, undimmed Ganchuk rosiness. When with an effort he stretched out his bent right arm, elbow first, and gripped your hand with his tenacious fingers, you felt a hint of his erstwhile strength. 'I am!' said his handshake, although his eyes were watering and he had difficulty with his speech. A pair of skis stood in a corner of the foyer. An old woman with a sharp, pointed nose and a head of neat grey curls came to help with the housework. One day I heard her singing softly in the kitchen.

Several times I visited Ganchuk with a tape recorder, in an attempt to extract from him some details about the noisy, abusive literary quarrels of the 1920s – there are almost no witnesses of those semi-legendary years still alive – but unfortunately I couldn't get much out of him. And not because the old man's memory was failing, but because he didn't want to remember. He wasn't interested any more. The events of those days were far more interesting to me than to him, and once he said with amazement and even some irritation: 'Good Lord, do you mean to say you found *that* article of mine too? I can't see why anyone wants to rummage around in all that nonsense . . .' On the other hand, he would talk with great enthusiasm about some mind-numbing soap opera that was running on TV, or about an article he had just read in *Science and Life*. He subscribed to eighteen different newspapers and magazines.

In October, on the anniversary of Sonya's death, we went to the cemetery. Sonya was buried in the grounds of the old crematorium, near the Donskoi Monastery. The crematorium had been closed eighteen months before; Moscow now burnt its dead somewhere else, out of town. People said that it was too far out, too inconvenient, too grim and forbidding. By contrast, the burial ground by the Donskoi Monastery was positively cosy. The cemetery was open to visitors until seven p.m., and it was ten minutes to seven when we arrived. The taxi waited for us in the little square in front of the gates. There was a mist on the ground, the trees and the cemetery wall were coal-black, but the sky still had a twilight glow and the place was alive with the cawing of rooks. We walked up to the entrance just as the gatekeeper was rattling an iron chain preparatory to locking the gates. I was leading the old man by the arm. The gatekeeper didn't want to let us in, and we started arguing in the darkness. We threatened, begged, tried to give him a tip, but the gatekeeper simply got ruder and more obstinate. Ganchuk pointed out that he was a state pensioner, that he was eighty-six and might die at any moment, but the gatekeeper shouted in a hoarse, angry voice that he was human too and wanted to get home on time.

'But you have no right, it's still ten minutes before closing time . . .'

'The grocery shops shut at a quarter to!'

'How can you compare the two things? Have you no conscience?'

'Don't you lecture me. I can compare what I like. Anyone would think comparisons were forbidden.'

'Tell me your name,' shouted Ganchuk weakly. 'Give me your name at once. I shall write a letter.'

'Prokhorov!' barked the gatekeeper. 'Lev Mikhailovich, if you want to know. So what? Where will you write to? The other world?'

'Shulepa,' I said quietly, 'let us in.'

The man, unrecognisable in the gloom, fell silent and stepped back from the gates. We walked in. Amid a silence punctuated by the noise of rooks, my heels crunched and Ganchuk's rubber galoshes shuffled over the asphalt. We moved very slowly; no doubt he travelled at about this pace when he went skiing. When we were about twenty paces past the gates, I said to Ganchuk, 'I think he used to be in our class. To hell with him.'

We skirted the black, inert crematorium and began looking for the grave, which took some time to find in the dark. The old man bent over and felt the gravestones. At last, breathing hard, he said, 'Here it is . . .'

He squatted on his haunches and spent a long time in that position, brushing, tidying, making the dead leaves rustle.

There can be nothing more terrible, I thought, than dead death. The extinguished crematorium was dead death. And Lev Shulepa at the gates of the cemetery . . . Suddenly I understood why the old man no longer wanted to recall the past. The rooks made a deafening noise as they circled and circled over our heads in great anger. It was as if we had invaded their kingdom. Or perhaps their hour had begun, the hour when we should not dare to go there. There were very many large, solid nests in the surrounding trees.

The old man whispered, as though talking to himself, 'What a pointless, idiotic world it is. Sonya's lying in the ground, her old friend refuses to let us in here, and I am eighty-six. Why? Who can explain it?' He gripped my arm with a prehensile claw. 'And yet how we long to stay in this world.'

Half an hour later we shuffled back to the entrance. The gates were wide open and the gatekeeper had disappeared. The taxi was still waiting for us. We drove in silence. It was not until we reached the square and turned into the tunnel leading to Sadovaya that Ganchuk leaned forward to the driver and asked him in a barely audible voice to go faster: there was a TV programme that he didn't want to miss. The traffic lights flashed, the lights began to come on all around, the city that I loved, remembered, knew, and tried to understand stretched out to infinity . . .

Soon afterwards, dressed in a worn-out leather jacket with a sheepskin collar, of the kind that airmen used to wear in the late forties, the gatekeeper came out onto the avenue leading past the monastery wall, turned left and emerged onto a broad thoroughfare, where he got on a trolleybus. Several minutes later, as he crossed the river by the bridge, he looked up at the long squat, ugly house on the embankment and out of habit picked out the windows of his old flat, in which he had spent his happiest years, and he wondered whether some miracle might happen and another change might take place in his life.

GABRIELA: CLOVE AND CINNAMON

JORGE AMADO

For Nacib, the Arab owner of the Vesuvius Bar in downtown Ilheus, Brazil, the discovery of the mulatto girl Gabriela, from the 'slave market' backlands, was a godsend; good cooks were hard to come by. Her food and her sensuous beauty were attracting more customers than ever before – and Nacib, too, fell helpless before her cinnamon skin and her fragrance of cloves. But marriage could not confine her, nor political intrigue contain her. And, whatever the disgrace she might bring, Nacib could not do without her . . .

JORGE AMADO is Brazil's best-loved writer, and a novelist of considerable international renown, whose books have been translated into over thirty languages. Awarded the Juca Pato prize in 1970, Amado's work includes TIETA and TEREZA BATISTA (both available in Abacus paperback).

'*An exciting and enjoyable romp.*' New York Times.

'*Displays all the positive qualities of Latin American fiction . . . As a story it has got it all: assassinations, political intrigues, treachery, vengeance, illicit liaisons, and, above all, a relentless narrative energy.*' Glasgow Herald.

'*Amado is by turns realist, fantastical, episodic, direct, angry, humorous, and, above all, characterful.*' Scotsman.

ABACUS FICTION   0 349 10074 8   £3.95

BABIES IN RHINESTONES
Shena Mackay

Enter the unsettling world of BABIES IN RHINESTONES – a world of deceptive appearances, where there are hidden traps and subtle revenge lurks, shadowed by thinly disguised menace.

Enter the world of Shena Mackay, whose highly individual stories present an unusual and distinctive picture of apparently ordinary events, and the darker causes which may lie at their roots . . .

'A rococo writer, noticing people and things with both murderous innocence and fantastical ingenuity . . . she captures moods and moments with sly accuracy.' *Observer*.

'There is an understated precision, a lethal accuracy of observation, about these stories which makes them impressive . . . a highly original talent.'
Times Literary Supplement.

'Tragic, pathetic and comic by turns . . . penetratingly accurate, relentless and yet compassionate. This is a very distinguished collection.'
Financial Times.

'Reading her stories is like walking on broken glass.' *Sunday Times*.

FICTION   0 349 122725   £2.75

Also available in ABACUS paperback:

FICTION

BABIES IN RHINESTONES	Shena Mackay	£2.75 ☐
THE STAMPING GROUND	Maurice Leitch	£2.75 ☐
BILGEWATER	Jane Gardam	£2.50 ☐
THE SEIZURE OF POWER	Czeslaw Milosz	£2.75 ☐
MORTAL MATTERS	Penelope Gilliatt	£2.95 ☐
BROTHERS	Bernice Rubens	£3.95 ☐
BETHANY	Anita Mason	£2.95 ☐
THE LAST TESTAMENT OF OSCAR WILDE	Peter Ackroyd	£2.50 ☐
TIME AND THE HUNTER	Italo Calvino	£2.50 ☐
IN COLD BLOOD	Truman Capote	£2.95 ☐

NON-FICTION

NAM	Mark Baker	£2.95 ☐
BLACK AND WHITE	Shiva Naipaul	£2.95 ☐
FROM HEAVEN LAKE	Vikram Seth	£2.50 ☐
SEX IN HISTORY	Reay Tannahill	£2.95 ☐
LETTERS FROM SACHIKO	James Trager	£2.75 ☐
MRS. HARRIS	Diana Trilling	£2.95 ☐
HITCH	John Russell Taylor	£2.75 ☐
MORTIMER WHEELER	Jacquetta Hawkes	£3.95 ☐
PETER THE GREAT	Robert K. Massie	£5.95 ☐
THE WILDER SHORES OF LOVE	Lesley Blanch	£2.95 ☐

All Abacus books are available at your local bookshop or newsagent, or can be ordered direct from the publisher. Just tick the titles you want and fill in the form below.

Name _____

Address _____

Write to Abacus Books, Cash Sales Department, P.O. Box 11, Falmouth, Cornwall TR10 9EN

Please enclose cheque or postal order to the value of the cover price plus:

UK: 55p for the first book plus 22p for the second book and 14p for each additional book ordered to a maximum charge of £1.75.

OVERSEAS: £1.00 for the first book plus 25p per copy for each additional book.

BFPO & EIRE: 55p for the first book, 22p for the second book plus 14p per copy for the next 7 books, thereafter 8p per book.

Abacus Books reserve the right to show new retail prices on covers which may differ from those previously advertised in the text or elsewhere, and to increase postal rates in accordance with the PO.